© Chris Saunders

About the Author

DORIS LESSING, winner of the 2007 Nobel Prize for Literature, is one of the most celebrated and distinguished writers of our time. She has been awarded the David Cohen Memorial Prize for British Literature, Spain's Prince of Asturias Prize and Prix Catalunya, and the S. T. Dupont Golden PEN Award for a Lifetime's Distinguished Service to Literature, as well as a host of other international awards. She lives in north London.

THE CLEFT

DORIS LESSING

The Cleft

HARPER ◉ PERENNIAL

NEW YORK • LONDON • TORONTO • SYDNEY • NEW DELHI • AUCKLAND

HARPER ● PERENNIAL

First published in Great Britain in 2007 by Fourth Estate, an imprint of HarperCollins Publishers.

A hardcover edition of this book was published in 2007 by HarperCollins Publishers.

HarperCollins books may be purchased for educational, business, or sales promotional use. For information please write: Special Markets Department, HarperCollins Publishers, 10 East 53rd Street, New York, NY 10022.

FIRST HARPER PERENNIAL EDITION PUBLISHED 2008.

The Library of Congress has catalogued the hardcover edition as follows:

Lessing, Doris May.
    The cleft / Doris Lessing.—1st U.S. ed.
        260 p. ; 22 cm.
    ISBN: 978-0-06-083486-9
    ISBN-10: 0-06-083486-2
    1. Sex (Psychology)—Fiction. 2. Creation—Fiction. 3. Women—
    Fiction. I. Title.
PR6023.E833 C57 2007b
823.914 22   2007298984

ISBN: 978-0-06-083487-6 (pbk.)

08 09 10 11 12   OFF/RRD   10 9 8 7 6 5 4 3 2 1

In a recent scientific article it was remarked that the basic and primal human stock was probably female, and that males came along later, as a kind of cosmic afterthought. I cannot believe that this was a trouble-free advent. The idea was grist to an already active mill, for I had been wondering if men were not a younger type, a junior variation. They lack the solidity of women, who seem to have been endowed with a natural harmony with the ways of the world. I think most people would agree with this, even if a definition would be hard to come by. Men in comparison are unstable, and erratic. Is Nature trying something out?

Brooding about this whole question sparked off speculation and then that spinning of the imagination that can lead to the birth of stories. Here is one of the tales about what might have happened when Clefts first gave birth to a baby boy.

Man does, woman is.

ROBERT GRAVES

Merchant
We travel not for trafficking alone:
By hotter winds our fiery hearts are fanned:
For lust of knowing what should not be known
We make the Golden Journey to Samarkand.

The Master of the Caravan
Open the gate, O watchman of the night.

The Watchman
Ho, travellers I open. For what land
Leave you the dim-moon city of delight?

The Merchants (WITH A SHOUT)
We make the Golden Journey to Samarkand.

(The caravan passes through the gate)

The Watchman (CONSOLING THE WOMEN)
What would you, ladies? It was ever thus.
Men are unwise and curiously planned.

A Woman
They have their dreams, and do not think of us.

Voices of the Caravan (IN THE DISTANCE, SINGING)
We make the Golden Journey to Samarkand.

JAMES ELROY FLECKER

THE CLEFT

I saw this today.

When the carts come in from the estate farm as the summer ends, bringing the wine, the olives, the fruits, there is a festive air in the house, and I share in it. I watch from my windows like the house slaves, for the arrival of the oxen as they turn from the road, listen for the creak of the cart. Today the oxen were wild-eyed and anxious, because of the noisy overfull road to the west. Their whiteness was reddened, just like the slave Marcus's tunic, and his hair was full of dust. The watching girls ran out to the cart, not only because of all the delicious produce they would now put away into the storerooms, but because of Marcus, who had in the last year become a handsome youth. His throat was too full of dust to let him return their greetings, and he ran to the pump, snatched up the pitcher there, drank – and drank – poured water over his head, which emerged from this libation a mass of black curls – and dropped the pitcher, through haste, on the tile surround, where it shattered. At this, Lolla,

whose mother my father had bought during a trip to
Sicily, an excitable explosive girl, rushed at Marcus
screaming reproaches and accusations. He shouted back,
defending himself. The other servants were already
lifting down the jars of wine and oil, and the grape
harvest, black and gold, and it was a busy, loud scene.
The oxen began lowing and now, and with an osten-
tatiously impatient air, Lolla took up a second pitcher,
dipped it in the water and ran with it to the oxen,
where she filled their troughs, which were nearly empty.
It was Marcus's responsibility to make sure the oxen
got their water as soon as they arrived. They lowered
their great heads and drank, while Lolla again turned
on Marcus, scolding and apparently angry. Marcus was
the son of a house slave in the estate house and these
two had known each other all their lives. Sometimes
he had worked here in our town house, sometimes she
had gone for the summer to the estate. Lolla was known
for her quick temper, and if Marcus had not been hot
and dusty after the long slow journey he would probably have laughed at her, teased her out of her fit of
impatience. But these two were no longer children: it
was enough only to see them together to know her
crossness, his sullenness, were not the result only of a
very hot afternoon.

He went to the oxen, avoiding their great tossing
horns, and began soothing them. He freed them from
their traces, and led them to the shade of the big fig
tree, where he slipped the traces over a branch. For
some reason Marcus's tenderness with the oxen annoyed

Lolla even more. She stood, watching, while the other girls were carrying past her the produce from the cart, and her cheeks were scarlet and her eyes reproached and accused the boy. He took no notice of her. He walked past her as if she were not there, to the veranda, where he pulled out another tunic from his bundle and, stripping off the dusty tunic, he again sluiced himself with water, and without drying himself – the heat would do that in a moment – he slipped on the fresh one.

Lolla seemed calmer. She stood with her hand on the veranda wall, and now she was penitent, or ready to be. Again he took no notice of her, but stood at the end of the veranda, staring at the oxen, his charges. She said, 'Marcus . . .' in her normal voice, and he shrugged, repudiating her. By now the last of the jars and the fruit had gone inside. The two were alone on the veranda. 'Marcus,' said Lolla again, and this time coaxingly. He turned his head to look at her, and I would not have liked to earn that look. Contemptuous, angry – and very far from the complaisance she was hoping for. He went to the gate to shut it, and turned from it, and from her. The slaves' quarters were at the end of the garden. He took up his bundle and began walking – fast, to where he would lodge that night. 'Marcus,' she pleaded. She seemed ready to cry. He was about to go into the men's quarters and she ran across and reached him as he disappeared into the door.

I did not need to watch any longer. I knew she would find an excuse to hang about the courtyard – perhaps petting and patting the oxen, giving them figs, or pretend the well needed attention. She would be waiting for him. I knew that he would want to go off into the streets with the other boys, for an evening's fun – he was not often here in this house in Rome itself. But I knew too that these two would spend tonight together, no matter what he would have preferred.

This little scene seems to me to sum up a truth in the relations between men and women.

Often seeing something as revealing, when observing the life of the house, I was impelled to go into the room where it was kept, the great pack of material which I was supposed to be working on. I had had it now for years. Others before me had said they would try to make something of it.

What was it? A mass of material accumulated over ages, originating as oral history, some of it the same but written down later, all purporting to deal with the earliest record of us, the peoples of our earth.

It was a cumbersome, unwieldy mass and more than one hopeful historian had been defeated by it, and not only because of its difficulty, but because of its nature. Anyone working on it must know that if it ever reached a stage of completion where it could have a name, and be known as a product of scholarship, it would be attacked, challenged, and perhaps be described as spurious.

I am not a person who enjoys the quarrels of scholars. What kind of a man I am is not really of importance in this debate – there has already been disputation about allowing this tale to exist away from the dusty shelves it has always been kept on. 'The Cleft' – I did not choose this title – had at various times been regarded as so inflammatory it had been put with other 'Strictly Secret' documents.

As I have said, the history I am relating is based on ancient documents, which are based on even earlier oral records. Some of the reported events are abrasive and may upset certain people. I tried out selected bits of the chronicle on my sister Marcella and she was shocked. She would not believe that decent females would be unkind to dear little baby boys. My sister is ever ready to ascribe to herself the more delicate of female attributes – a not uncommon trait, I think. But as I remind her, anyone who has watched her screaming her head off as the blood flows in the arena is not likely easily to be persuaded of female fastidiousness. People wishing to avoid offence to their sensibilities may start the story on p.29.

The following is not the earliest bit of history we have, but it is informative and so I am putting it first.

Yes, I know, you keep saying, but what you don't understand is that what I say now can't be true because I am telling you how I see it all now, but it was all different then. Even words I use are new, I don't know where they came from, sometimes it seems that most of the words in our mouths are this new talk. I say I, and again I, I do this and I think that, but *then* we wouldn't say I, it was we. We thought we.

I say *think* but did we think? Perhaps a new kind of thinking began like everything else when the Monsters started being born. I am sorry, you keep saying the truth, you want the truth, and that is how we saw you, all of you, at first. Monsters. The deformed ones, the freaks, the cripples.

When was then? I don't know. *Then* was a very long time ago, that's all I know.

The caves are old. You have seen them. They are old caves. They are high in the rocks, well above any waves, even big ones, even the biggest. In stormy seas you can stand on the cliffs and look down and think that water is everything, is everywhere, but then the storm stops and the sea sinks back into its place. We are not afraid of the sea. We are sea people. The sea made us. Our caves are warm, with sandy floors, and dry, and the fires outside each cave burn sea-brush and dry seaweed and wood from the cliffs, and these fires have never gone out, not since we first had them. There was a time we didn't have fire. That is in our records. Our story is known. It is told to chosen youngsters and they have to remember it and tell it when they are old to new youngsters. They have to be sure they remember every word, as it was told to them.

What I am saying now is not part of this kind of recording. When the story is told to the young ones – they have a name, they are called the Memories –

it is told first among ourselves, and one will say, 'No, it was not like that,' or another, 'Yes, it was like that,' and by the time everyone is agreed we can be sure there is nothing in the story that is untrue.

You want to know about me? Very well, then. My name is Maire. There is always someone called Maire. I was born into the family of Cleft Watchers, like my mother and like her mother – these words are new. If everyone gives birth, as soon as they are old enough, everyone is a mother, and you don't have to say Mother. The Cleft Watchers are the most important family. We have to watch The Cleft. When the moon is at its biggest and brightest we climb up to above The Cleft where the red flowers grow, and we cut them, so there is a lot of red, and we let the water flow from the spring up there, and the water flushes the flowers down through The Cleft, from top to bottom, and we all have our blood flow. That is, all who are not going to give birth. Very well, have it your way, the moon's rays make the blood flow, not the red running down through The Cleft. But we *know* that if we don't cut the red flowers – they are small and soft like the blisters on seaweed, and they bleed red if you crush them – if we don't do that, we will not have our flow.

The Cleft is that rock there, which isn't the entrance to a cave, it is blind, and it is the most important thing in our lives. It has always been so. We are The

Cleft, The Cleft is us, and we have always made sure it is kept free of saplings that might grow into trees, free of bushes. It is a clean cut down through the rock and under it is a deep hole. Every year, when the sun touches the top of that mountain there, it is always the cold time, and we have killed one of us, and thrown the body down from the top of The Cleft into the hole. You say you have counted the bones, but I don't see how you can have, when some of the bones are dust by now. You say if a body and its bones has been thrown down every year, it is not so difficult to work out how long it has been going on. Well, if that is what you think is important . . .

No, I cannot say how it started. That isn't in our story.

The Old Shes must have known something.

We never called them that before the Monsters began being born. Why should we? We only had Shes, didn't we, only Clefts, and as for *old*, we didn't think like that. People were born, they lived for a time, unless they drowned swimming or had an accident or were chosen to be thrown into The Cleft. When they died they were put out on the Killing Rock.

No, I don't know how many of us there were *then*. Whenever then was. There are these caves, as many as I have fingers and toes, and they are big and they go back a long way into the cliffs. Each cave has the same kind of people in it, a family, the Cleft Watchers,

the Fish Catchers, the Net Makers, the Fish Skin
Curers, the Seaweed Collectors. And that is what we
were called. My name was Cleft Watcher. No, why
did it matter if several people had the same name?
You can always tell by looking at someone, can't
you?

My name Maire is one of the new words.

We didn't think like that, no, we didn't, that every
person had to have a name separate from all the
others. Sometimes I think we lived in a kind of dream,
a sleep, everything slow and easy and nothing ever
happening but the moon being bright and big, and
the red flowers washing down The Cleft.

And, of course, the babies being born. They were
just born, that's all, no one did anything to make
them. I think we thought the moon made them, or
a big fish, but it is hard to remember what we thought,
it was such a dream. How we thought has never been
part of our story, only what happened.

You get angry when I say Monsters, but just look
at yourself. Look at yourself – and look at me. Go
on, look. I am not wearing the red flower belt so you
can see how I am. Now look at The Cleft, we are
the same, The Cleft and the Clefts. No wonder you
cover yourselves there, but we don't have to. We are
nice to look at, like one of those shells we can pick
off a rock after a storm. *Beautiful* – you taught us
that word and I like to use it. I am beautiful, just

11

like The Cleft with its pretty red flowers. But you are all bumps and lumps and the thing like a pipe which is sometimes like a sea squirt. Can you wonder that when the first babes like you were born we put them out for the eagles?

We always used to throw deformed babies there, on that rock, the sloping rock just past The Cleft itself. One side of The Cleft rises out of the Killing Rock, yes, that's what we call it. We didn't keep damaged babies, and we didn't keep twins. We were careful to limit our numbers because it was better that way. Why was it? Because that's how it has always been, and we never thought to change things. We did not have a lot of births, perhaps two or three to a cave in a long time, and sometimes a cave had no babies at all in it. Of course we are pleased when a baby is born, but if we kept all the babes born there would be no room for us all. Yes, I know you say we should find a bit of shore where there is more room, but we have always been here, and how could we move from The Cleft? This is our place, it has always been ours.

When we put out deformed babies the eagles came for them. We did not kill the babes, the eagles did it. An eagle keeps watch on that peak over there – can you see it? That little speck there, it is a great big eagle, the size of a person. We put out all the newborn Monsters and watched as the eagles carried them off to their nests. That time went on, we believe, and it went on, because the Old Shes (your name for them) were worried because there were so many fewer in the caves, so many Monsters had been born, more than babes like us, the females.

Males, females. New words, new people.

And it went on, instead of waiting for a birth with pleasure, we were afraid, and when one of us saw that the babe was a Monster, she was ashamed and the others hated her. Not for ever, of course, but it was a terrible thing, the moment when a Monster appeared at the moment of giving birth. There were fewer of us catching fish and gathering seafood. The Old Shes were complaining they were not getting enough to eat. Yes, we always fed them and gave them the nicest bits to eat. I don't know why, we just did. Suddenly there were only half the number in the Fish Catchers' cave, and some of the others who were not Fish Catchers had to become Catchers.

I agree, it was strange we never thought to wonder what was happening on the other side of the Eagles' Hills. You always talk as if we are stupid, but if we are so stupid how is it we have lived for so long, safely and well, so much longer than you, the Monsters, have. Our story goes back and back, you tell us so, but your story is much shorter. But why should we have moved about and looked for new things, or wondered about the eagles? What for? We

13

have everything we want on this part of the island –
your word for it, you tell us it is a large island. Well,
good for you, but what difference does that make to
us? We live in the part of the island where we watch
the sun drop into the sea every night, and watch the
moon grow pale as day comes.

A long time after the first Monster was born, we
saw down on that part of the seashore nearest to the
Eagles' Hills one of the Monsters, one of you. It had
tied around its waist one of the fish-skin cloths we
wear at the time of the red flower. We could see that
under the skin was the lumpy swelling thing we
thought was so ugly. This was a Monster we had
given birth to, grown up. How had that happened?
The Old Shes said we should lie in wait and kill that
Monster next time it appeared on the shore. Then
there was disagreement among the Old Shes, and
some said we should climb up to the hills where the
eagles lived next time we put out a Monster to die,
and watch where the eagles took it. And some of us
did that. They were very afraid, that is in the story
we make the youngsters learn. We were not in the
habit of roaming about and certainly never as far as
the Eagles' Hills. No one had gone so far before. Yes,
I know it is not more than a comfortable walk.

They saw the eagle carry the Monster in its claws
up to the hills where the nests are but instead of dropping the baby in a nest the eagle went on and carried

the baby down into a valley where there are huts. We had never seen a hut or any shelter because we had always had our caves. The huts seemed like some kind of strange animal, and very nearly frightened us into running back home. The eagle took the baby down, and then some Monsters took it and gave the bird a big lump of food. We know now it was a fish. The babe was taken into a hut. Everything they saw frightened the Watchers, and they did run home and told the Old Shes what they had seen. It was a terrible, frightening story they told. Over the Eagles' Hills were living Monsters, grown people, not Clefts like us. They were able to live though they were so deformed and ugly. That is how we thought then. Everyone was afraid, and shocked, and didn't know what to think or what to do.

Then another Monster was born and the Old Shes told us to throw it over that cliff there into the sea. A group of us took the babe to the clifftop. They did not want to kill it, because they knew now it could grow up and live and if they threw it into the waves that would kill it. All of us swim and float and are happy in the sea, but our babes have to be taught. They were crying and wailing and the babe was yelling, because they were out of earshot of the Old Shes there and they were so divided about what they were doing. They hated the Monsters, and now they were afraid, too, since they knew about the Monsters living over the hills . . . look, you asked me to tell you what happened, so why get angry when I do? How do you know, if some of us Clefts had been born into your community, you might have thought we were Monsters because we are different. Yes, I know you can't give birth, only we Clefts can give birth, and you despise us, yes, you do, but without us there would be no Monsters, there would be *no one at all*. Have you ever thought of that? We Clefts make all the people, Clefts and Monsters. If there were no Clefts, what would happen – have you really thought about that?

They were standing on the cliff with the yelling baby Monster when one of the big eagles appeared floating just above them, and it screamed and screamed at them, and now they were really afraid. The eagles are so big they can carry a grown person – not very far, but it could have lifted one of those of us on the cliff, perhaps the one holding the babe, up and over and into the sea. Or those great wings could knock them one by one into the waves that were crashing and jumping in the sharp rocks. But what happened was not that. The eagle let itself down from the sky and took the baby in its claws and went off with it back in the direction of the Eagles' Hills.

The Clefts didn't know what to do. They were

afraid to tell the Old Shes what had happened. I don't remember anyone saying anything about being afraid before.

Then a new thing began. When a Monster was born, the young ones pretended to throw it away into the waves, but they went far away so they could not be seen, and knew that the babe's crying would fetch an eagle. Then they laid the babe down on the cliff and watched while the eagle swept down and took it. By then as many Monsters were being born as Clefts, the ones like us, the ones like you.

Have you ever thought how strange it is that you have nipples on those flat places in front there? You can't call them breasts, can you? Why have nipples at all when they aren't good for anything? You can't feed a babe with them, they are useless.

Yes, I am sure you have thought, because you are always noticing things and asking questions. Well, what is your reply, then?

Next, an Old She said we should keep one of the Monsters, one of you, and let it grow and see if it was fit for anything.

It was hard to do because the eagles watched us all the time, and we had to keep the baby Monster out of their sight.

I don't really like to think of what happened to that babe. Of course I only heard about it all, it was part of the story, it was told again and again by the

Memories, and what I am telling you now is only some of what we called the story.

There is a bad feeling about that part of our story. There were disagreements, worse, bad quarrels. It is in the story that there had never been that kind of quarrel before. Some Old Shes wanted not to tell about the first monstrous babe and how it was treated. Others said what was the point of the story if it left bits out? I believe a lot was left out. What we all know is that, first of all, no one wanted to feed the Monster. It was never fed enough and it was always hungry and crying. That meant that the eagles were always hovering about trying to see where we kept the babe. It did get fed, but the one feeding it would tease and torment it as it fed. That first Monster babe had a bad time.

Then one of the Shes said it must stop, either we decided to let it live and look after it, or not, but what was happening now would kill the babe. What did we do to it? The thing you all have in front, the lumps and the tube was what everyone wanted to play with. The little Monster screamed and screamed and its lumps were swollen and became sick and full of matter and bad-smelling water. Then one of the Old Shes said that the Monsters were really like us, except for your thing in front, and your flat breasts. It was like one of our babies. Cut off the thing in front and see what happens – well, they did cut it off and it died. All the time it screamed and howled and when another Monster was born and it was kept, it was a little better treated but I don't want to tell you everything about how these little Monsters were treated. And I think that some of us became ashamed. We are not cruel people. There is no record of any of us doing cruel things – not until the Monsters were born. The Monster we were trying to bring up strayed outside the cave we kept it in and a watching eagle swept down at once and took it over the hill to the others. How they survived, those babes, we have no idea.

Then there were quite a few Monsters born all at once. Some of the Old Shes wanted us to keep another for a plaything, others not. But the story goes that quite a few of the babes were put out on the Killing Rock at the same time and instead of one eagle, or two, as many came as there were little Monsters, and we watched as the babes were carried off and over the hills. How did those babes live? Babies need milk. There is a tale that one of our young Clefts became sorry for the hungry babes, and went by herself over the hills and found the new babes crawling about and crying, and she fed as many as she could. There is always milk in our breasts. Our breasts are useful. Not like yours.

And she stayed there with the Monsters, but no one knows now what really happened. We want to believe it, I think, because we are ashamed of the rest of the story, but there is also the question, how did those babies live when they were not fed?

There is a tale that two of us were sitting by the sea, watching the waves and sometimes sliding in for a little swim, then they saw two of the fish we call breast fish, because that is what they look like, big puffy jellies, and they have tubes sticking out, like the Monsters, and one of them stuck his tube into the other, and there were little eggs scattering through the water.

That was when the idea first happened to us that the Monsters' tubes were for making eggs, and if so why and what for?

This tale, I think, is fanciful, but something like that, I suppose, happened.

The Old Shes began to talk about it, because we told them – by 'we' there I mean the young ones, who found something intriguing about those tubes and the eggs. Some of the young ones went over the hill and when the Monsters saw them, they grabbed them and put their tubes into them, and that is how we became Hes and Shes, and learned to say I as well as we – but after that there are several stories, not one. Yes, I know what I am telling you doesn't add up to sense but I told you, there are many stories and who knows which one is true? And some time after that, we, the Clefts, lost the power to give birth without them, the Monsters – without you.

This account, by this Maire, was later than the first document we have. Much later – ages. Ages is a word to be distrusted: it means there is no real knowledge. It is a smooth tale, told many times and even the remorse for cruelty has something well-used about it. No, it's not untrue, it is useful, as far as it goes, but a lot has been left out. What that is, is in the first document, or fragment, which is probably the very first attempt at 'the story'. It is crude, unaccomplished, and told by someone in shock. Before the birth of the first 'Monsters' nothing had ever happened – not in ages – to this community of first humans. The first Monster was seen as an unfortunate birth fault. But then there was another, and another . . . and the realisation that it was all going to continue. And the Old Females were in a panic, raging, screaming, punishing the young females who were producing the Monsters, and their treatment of the Monsters themselves – well, it does not make for pleasant reading, Maire's account, but I cannot bring myself to reproduce that other fragment here. It is too unpleasant. I am a Monster and cannot help identifying with those long-ago tortured infants, the first baby boys. The ingenuity of the cruelties thought up by the Old Females is sickening. Even now, the period of putting the newborn out to die, then keeping a few, and mutilating them – well, it went on much longer than the account above suggests. Very much longer.

Something like a war developed between the eagles and the first females, who could not possibly win. Not only were they unused to fighting, or even aggression, they were unused to physical activity. They lay around on their rocks and they swam. That was their life, had been for – ages. And suddenly here were these great angry birds, who watched every move they made, and tried to wrest the Monsters from them as they were born. Some of the females, the young ones attending to the Monsters, were killed – swept into the sea and then kept from climbing out because the eagles hovered above them and pushed them under until they drowned. This war could not go on for long but it created the females' first enemy. They hated the eagles, and for a time tried to hurt them by throwing stones, or beating at them with sticks. Not only fear, but elementary forms of attack and defence began in this sleepy (Maire's word) community of the very first humans, the very first females. And this was in itself enough to throw the Old Females, who ruled them, off balance. They became almost as much to be feared as the eagles, and the young women banded together and threatened their elders with harm. After all, it was they who gave birth to the Monsters, had to feed them, if it was decided this one or that would be kept, or whether to get rid of them. It was they who were given that nasty task. The Old Females lay shrieking or moaning on the rocks, railing at anything and everything.

The coming of the Monsters not only shocked the first females out of their long dream, but nearly ended it. They had to stop fighting each other, because not every young mother hated the Monsters enough to destroy them. There was a churning and wallowing and upheaving of emotions, and that nearly did for them, in a kind of civil war.

I am writing this, feeling some of those ancient long-ago emotions. I note that Maire in her account said 'we' and 'us' identifying with the first Clefts, just as I cannot help identifying with the very first males. It is sickening to read the fragment that tells of the little Monsters. Even now, to read how the old ones ordered the young to cut off the 'tubes and lumps' of the babes, which of course killed them, and how they exulted – even now, it is painful. I shall spare you, I shall not reproduce the fragment. After all they, the females, decided not to include it in their official story, the one they taught to their Memories. Why then do we have this fragment? We have to deduce that there was a minority opinion, which did not approve of the truth being suppressed – the revolting, sickening truth. Someone, or a group, kept the fragment, and someone, or several, taught words to a Memory. A long time passed, while this sickening little tale was told, 'mouth to ear', our name for our oral histories, to generation after generation, and it was never incorporated into the main story. And then?

And then there was a point when all the verbal preserved tales were written down, in an ancient language which only recently has been deciphered. The seditious damaging addendum to the official story was always written separately, and that is why the earlier decipherers believed it to be a fraud, something written by males to discredit the whole female sex. But there is something too raw and bleeding about the account of the cruelties to be a fake. There are details that I don't think it would have been easy to fake.

And who is this historian? I am a scribe and researcher, known for my interest in the unusual, the out of the way. My name for this book is 'Transit'. What my real name is I shall keep dark. This parcel or packet of scrolls containing the story of the Clefts and the Monsters has been on the back shelves of libraries, or languishing in scholars' shelves, for a long time. A good many people have read the story and no one has been unmoved by it. There have been copies made, for that kind of person who sees everything as pornography.

Shameful history preserved on ancient shards is by no means the only dangerous information kept locked up.

This is the place for an explanation. All this locking up and smoothing over and the *suppression of the truth* took place when it was agreed all hostilities were over and we were One – one Race, or People. With so much unhappy history in our memories, and much of it preserved in the Official Memories, *it was agreed* – this formulation always signals the smoothing over of disagreement – that as much of the inflammatory material as could be got together must be put in a safe place, and made inaccessible to anyone but the trusted custodians.

Of whom I am – I was – one. And this is the next part of the explanation. Why am I in a position to tell you about this material? It is because I have preserved, guarded and watched over it now for a long time.

I am establishing my credentials here, right at the beginning of my story. What I am about to relate may be – must be – speculative, but it is solidly based on fact. I have put right at the beginning fragments of what has been locked up, to give a flavour of the material I have had to work with. You may say that the account is not consistent. But we are talking about events so long ago, no one now can say how long. And this has an interesting aspect. It is a record of an interrogation by one of us – that is, the males (or Monsters, to make use of a still current joke) – of a She, or Cleft. This is in itself enough to make one stop and wonder. No doubt at all that the interrogator is in a position of power, and that locates the event late in our long history. But it was preserved by the method used by the females, the memorising of a history, an account, preserved in the memories of the Memory, and passed on down to the succeeding generations of Memories. So we are talking about very early events indeed, when we look at a later preserved, but still very early, tale which has little in common with what is taught our children as the truth. Which is, of course, that we males were first in the story and in some remarkable way brought forth the females. *We* are the senior, *they* our creation. Interesting indeed when you look at the anatomies, male and female. How, in our official story, is it explained that males have no apparatus for bringing forth and nurturing? It is not explained. We have attractive and hazy fables, created at the same time as the great Locking Up – and, I am afraid, often destroying – of documents.

But you cannot destroy what is preserved in people's minds. The method used by the females, the careful repetition, word by word, and then the handing down to the next generation, every word compared and checked, by a method of parallel Lines of Memories, is a very efficient preserver of history. For as long as the checking and comparing continues. You would be surprised at the mass of material in our – I jokingly called them prisons. Yes, this, I am afraid, is the joke used by us official warders of the forbidden truth. Nearly all of it came from the female Memories, though, when we began to use the same process, from our Memories too. Though, officially, *they* took the process from us. Absurd. It is the sheer absurdity of our official version that has become such a heavy burden on us, the historians.

No one has undertaken the task of studying the material as a serious record, and then attempting to make a coherent history. Myths and legends are more the province of the Greeks, and this could be presented as a legend, but no Greek has taken on the task. That is probably because this is not a legend, but some kind of factual story. Our own history does not go back so very far, does it? And it too bursts forth out of myth, with Aeneas, and the flames from burning Troy illuminating our earliest time, just as they do the Greeks'.

Perhaps it has been felt that an account of our beginnings that makes females the first and founding stock is unacceptable. In Rome now, a sect – the Christians – insist that the first female was brought forth from the body of a male. Very suspect stuff, I think. Some male invented that – the exact opposite of the truth.

I have always found it entertaining that females are worshipped as goddesses, while in ordinary life they are kept secondary and thought inferior. Perhaps this tendency of mine to scepticism has made me able to take on the task of telling the tale of our real origins which, as you will see, does have elements of legend. Those eagles, for instance, the persecutors of the first females, the saviours of the first males. Well, we in Rome cannot criticise a tendency to make a fetish of eagles – even if ours are so much smaller than the great eagles of the Clefts and the Monsters.

> We are the Eagles, the Eagle, the Children of the Eagle. The Eagles bore us on their wings, they bear us on their breath, they are the wings of the wind, the Great Eagle watches us, he knows us, he is our Father, he hates our enemies, he fights for us against the Clefts.

Note by Historian: This is the dancing song of the Very First Men, and it may be heard even now, its origins long forgotten, sung in remote places. The Eagle people continue the strongest clan, the rulers. Even now anyone killing an eagle must be punished: once they were immediately put to death.

Here is a war chant of the Very First Men:

> Kill the Clefts,
> Kill them, kill them,
> They are our enemies
> Kill them all.

On ceramics as old as anything we have are pictures of genital mutilation, by no means only of males by females, but of females by males. These are not the sophisticated jars and vessels of an era considered to be of artistic merit. They are clumsy and rough. Depictions of torture are kept locked up and most people don't know of their existence. Some ruler of an optimistic cast of temperament decreed all depictions of tortures of any kind must be destroyed or kept locked up: apparently believing that we humans would be incapable of cruelty if the ideas weren't first put into our heads. I wonder who he was. Or, perhaps it was a She. A long time ago. The hoard of pottery was found in a cave that it is suspected was a dwelling place for primitives.

So, I shall end the explanations and come to my attempt at a history; one that both Clefts and Monsters, males and females, would agree to. Immediately I confront a problem. I wrote there 'males and females'. Males are always put first, in our practice. They are first in our society, despite the influence of certain great ladies of the noble Houses. Yet I suspect this priority was a later invention.

THE HISTORY

Compiled from ancient verbal records, written down many ages after their collection.

They lay on rocks, the waves splashing them, like seals, like sick seals, because they are pale and seals are mostly black. At first we thought they were seals. Singing seals? We had never heard seals sing, though some say they have heard them. Then we knew they were the Clefts. There were three of us boys. We knew we hated the Clefts though we did not remember anything of our earliest days, of being put out on the Killing Rock, or being carried over the mountain by the eagles. What we were seeing had to surprise, no matter what we had been told. More, we were disgusted. Those large pale *things* rolling in the waves, with their disgusting clefts, which we saw for the first time, and as we looked, from the cleft of one of those slow lolling creatures emerged a bloody small-sized thing. We saw it was a tiny Cleft. Only later did we reason that it might just as well have been a Squirt – one of us. We ran back, past the big Cleft in the cliffs, with its reddish stains and fuzzy growths. We ran and we vomited and we went back up the mountain and over down to our place.

This above is the earliest account we have of how we 'Monsters' saw the 'Clefts'. There is no way of proving it but I would say it is a memory of something well in the past of the speaker. It has the smoothed-over much-repeated quality of a tale from long ago. There is nothing here like the raw angry fragment (which I did not copy out because of its relishing vindictive cruelty) which is the very first we hear from the Clefts.

To make a history from this kind of material is not easy, but I have to say in justification that seldom did the Memories of the Clefts and Monsters differ very much. Often the tone was different, and once it was believed that different events were being recorded. But on the whole Clefts and Monsters (or Squirts) lived the same story. Now I again begin my tale.

They lived on the shore of a warm sea on an island that was in fact very large, but they never went far from home shore. They were of the sea, sea creatures, eating fish and seaweeds and some shore-growing fruits. They used tall caves with sandy floors but they might as easily sleep out on the rocks as under the cave roofs. How long had they lived there? And at once we come to a main difficulty – indeed, this historian's main problem. The Clefts did not know when their kind had first crawled from the waves to breathe air on the rocks, and they were incurious. They did not think to wonder or ask questions. They met the query – but this came much later – 'How old are you, as a people?' with bland, blind enquiry: 'What do you mean?' Their minds were not set for questions, even a mild interest. They believed – but it was not a belief they would defend or contest – that a Fish brought them from the Moon. When was that? Long, slow, puzzled stares. They were hatched from the moon's eggs. The moon laid eggs into the sea, it lost a part of itself, and that was why it was sometimes large and glowing and sometimes pale and thin. As for their own capacity to give birth, they had never questioned it. That was how things had always been. Nothing changed, could change, would change – but this was more a feeling than something they could or would enlarge on or even mention. They lived in an eternal present. *For how long?* Useless to ask. When the first 'Monster' was born it was seen merely as one of the deformed babes that had sometimes to occur, and then there was another 'Monster' all shaped in the same horrid and disturbing way. They were put out on the Killing Rock, not fed to the fishes, perhaps, because of a superstitious feeling that in the sea the Monsters might proliferate and even crawl back to the shore. Can we use the word 'superstition' about creatures who did not live in any kind of reality we would recognise?

I believe the birth of the Monsters was the first bad or even disturbing thing to have happened to them.

Yes, there were high water-line marks on their cave walls, big waves must at some time have come rushing up, more than once, but these were creatures of the sea. There is no way of finding out what they felt about monster waves – their songs are not histories or stories but a kind of keening, sounding like the wind when it sighs and murmurs.

It was not the first Monster that shocked them out of their dream. A twisted arm or leg, a deformed hand, even blurred features or a misshapen head – that kind of thing was sad but not threatening, as when they saw the second or third or succeeding babes with the clutch of protruding flesh there in front where they had smooth flesh, a neat slit, fringed with soft hair. A horror . . . and then another . . . and then another . . . they could not wait to get these misborn babes out on to the Killing Rock. Those squirting protruding things there in front, which changed shape all the time, oh horrid, ugly, there was something about them that . . .

Well, the eagles carried them off and ate them, took them out of sight.

But everything had changed. It must have been the

same as when you poke with a stick one of those torpid stranded beach creatures, which squirms as it feels the stick.

Shock after shock was felt by this community of dreaming creatures and it was their helpless panic that caused their cruelty.

And when it became evident that the Monsters were not going to stop appearing there was this new threat, that the numbers of the community were always reducing.

And there was fear that some female who had given birth to a Monster would then have another. How would she have been viewed? There is no record anywhere of early animosity among these creatures. Was she feared? Did she fear herself? Did a female who had given birth to more than one Monster procure for herself an abortion when finding again that she was pregnant? We have no answers to these questions.

How long did that early time last?

There is no help for us in the Memories.

There is a way of not measuring, but getting a feel of the long process. The deep grave or pit where the girls were sacrificed was crammed with bones, and it was a deep hole. At its bottom were cracks and apertures where rocks had fallen outwards, and through these could be glimpsed the lower layers of bones, not fresh and whole, like the top layers, but fractured and fragmented, and lower down still, on the floor of this great hole was a layer of whitish stuff, the dust of bones. It was a deep layer. It must have taken a long time for these bones to turn to dust, even though winds and salty wet blew into the holes and gaps, hastening the process.

It was not likely that these people who seemed to live in a dream were regular in their sacrificing, or regular in anything; impulses and rhythms we may hardly guess at governed their lives. But while there was no way of counting the skeletons or making an estimate of what the dust layers meant in terms of time, we may confidently say that we are talking of long periods of time – ages.

Of changelessness, of an existence like those fish that wash back and forth on the tides, responding to the moon's changes. And then the real change, the defining change, the birth of the deformed ones, the Squirts, the Monsters. The beginning of squirming emotional discomfort, unrest, discontent: the start of awareness of themselves, their lives. The start only, like the affront the stranded fish must feel at the probing stick.

There is a part of this tale that has to remain dark. Yes, yes, previous attempts at solving the mystery have offered solutions more like myths than probabilities. How did the community of males begin? We cannot believe that the eagles fed the infants regurgitated raw meat and kept them warm in their feathers. No, there is a solution and this is it.

The defective infants put out on the Killing Rock were for – how long? – food for the eagles. And the very first Monsters must have been too. But then – but when we don't know – boys kept as 'pets' and playthings by the Clefts escaped. We know that small boys as young as four, certainly aged five, six, seven, can achieve feats of endurance and even of strength. Two, three, four little boys ran away from the caves above the sea. The eagles, though they were very big, many times the size of the eagles we know, could not have carried children that size, not for fair distances. The children saw where the eagles flew back, to their nests, past the Killing Rock, over the valley, up the mountain – and they followed. Up on the ridge, where the eagles' nests were, they did not linger. How terrifying those enormous birds must have been. Down the other side and into the valley where the great river was. The children had been reared on fish, and here were fish again, though different ones. They had been kept warm in the caves. But they were still little children, and how very large the valley they found themselves in must have seemed. How can we not admire them for their daring and their cleverness? The river was wide, deep, and rushed along. Yet they had to catch fish in it. How did they shelter? It did not at once become possible to make huts and sheds:

they had never seen anything like them. They had
seen the eagles' nests and they dragged sticks and
then larger sticks and made piles of them, and crept
into them when dark came. Then they grew bigger
and stronger and they began leaning fallen branches
together to make shelters. This was an easy climate;
they did not have to fear cold. But let us not forget
the beasts in the forests that stood at a distance on
either side of the great river. How they escaped the
beasts has to remain a bit of a marvel. Did some god
or goddess aid the little things? But in their records
is never the mention of divine intervention. Yes, they
were the children of the Eagle, but that is as far as
divinity went, for them.

We must remember the first little males were badly
mutilated, in ways I for one would rather not dwell
on. Their 'squirts' had been so mishandled, pulled
and played with, and their sacs had sometimes been
cut off for the game of extracting the stones, and
above all, they had never known tenderness or
maternal care. Their mothers had fed them, on the
orders of the Old Shes, but reluctantly, and never
enough. We may like to soften this painful story by
imagining a Cleft who did feel some affection for her
misbegotten babe, but she would have had to hide
what she felt, and any caresses or care must have
been sketchy. And they were tough, and hardy and
skilful at avoiding attention. Skinny little boys, but

strong and fearless, improbably surviving, but at least they were away from their tormentors, the Clefts.

Then something remarkable happened. The eagles brought them some boy babies, left out on the Killing Rock. Hungry yelling babies, but not mutilated; and how were the little boys to feed them?

Not only dangerous wild animals lived in the forests, friendly ones did too. The little boys saw deer, with fawns and probably had their first lessons in parental love, watching does with their fawns. They crept close, to watch. A doe stood its ground, unafraid: there was no reason yet for any animal to fear our kind. And besides, this was a child, and needy. The boy stood fondling the doe's soft fur, while the fawn butted or licked his legs. Then the fawn began to suckle. And the boy, kneeling, did the same. The doe stood, and turned her head and licked the child. And so that was how began the intimacy between the children and the deer.

There was a song, 'We are the children of the deer', but it was never as compelling as the songs about the eagles.

When the new babies howled and screamed and the little boys knew they had to be fed, what could have been more natural than for the babes to be taken to the does, who had soon to learn to lie down, the babes beside them. And what did the does gain from this? We may speculate. It is my belief that animals are more intelligent than we ever give them credit for. After all, it was a she wolf who suckled our fore-fathers, Romulus and Remus. Her statue and the two babes are much loved by us. Probably the beginning of this bond was the terrible need of the babes, who were dying for lack of what the deer – and the she wolf – had in plenty. Need calls forth its response.

And why did the eagles take to saving the babes and bringing them over the mountain to the lads, instead of devouring them? For one thing, the boys caught fish for the eagles, and laid them on the grass, and the great birds, having delivered their burden of screaming babies, would stand over the fish, enor-mous fish, and feed there, and often they came between deliveries of babes, for their meals. Or they would take a fish or part of one – there were very large fish in the river – up into the mountain for their nestlings.

And the second wave of Monsters, or Squirts, were not mother-deprived, but were licked and nuzzled and fed by the kindly deer, who sometimes played with the fawns as if they were fawns themselves.

The feeding babies and deer would have to lie down together. There were no vessels or containers then. Soon, though, shells from the river became utensils, and gourds. There was not nearly as much weed in the river as there was in the sea, but these boys grew into strong lads, and the seashore was not far for hardy boys. This shore was a distance from the Clefts' shore, but continuous with it. The boys did not know for a long time that if they had journeyed in one direction along their beaches – they had beaches, the Clefts only had smooth warm rocks – they would encounter the Clefts, their persecutors.

They brought varieties of weed from the sea, and shellfish, and some sea fish, and the new babes were fed very well, as soon as they outgrew milk. And the friendly deer were offered weed, which they liked, and flesh of the fish and shellfish, but this they did not like.

But it must have been hard for the boys, keeping the babes fed, even with the aid of the deer. The eagles were always bringing more of the Monsters and these were not mutilated now. The eagles were perched on high rocks from where they could see the Clefts and their rocks, and as soon as there was a new little boy, they swooped and saved it and brought it over the mountain.

Some Squirts, we believe, were still hidden in the caves, but you cannot easily keep prisoner energetic boys, unless they are tied. Some Squirts were tied, but they made such a noise, yelling and screaming, that when they escaped, running away, guided by the great birds, the old Clefts were relieved. No more little boys were kept as 'pets', and the Clefts reverted to their earlier practice: any babe not snatched away by the eagles as they came out of the womb were put out on the Killing Rock and instantly carried off by the eagles.

Soon there was a community of young males, we do not know how many. The chroniclers did not go in for exactitude. And time was passing, the very first arrivals were now strong young men, and troubled with all kinds of questions about their equipment of tubes and bumps and lumps. Yes, they knew now the tube was for passing urine.

The males could not expect to live till old age, not when they were in and out of that dangerous rushing river, and the wild animals were so close in the trees. One died, of an illness, or of an accident, and the chroniclers did not specify; what they recorded was that this death raised a question . . . they saw that they could expect to die, and then what would they do to replace themselves? The Clefts had the power of birth, but they did not.

As for the Squirts – and I like that term better than the Monsters: at least it is accurate – they began to be anxious about the supply of babes brought by the eagles. Suppose the eagles decided not to bring the boy babies over the mountain? Once the question had arisen it would not go away. Over there on their shore – and some of the boys remembered it well – the Clefts gave birth. Without the Clefts there would be no new arrivals in the eagles' claws, there would be no Squirts.

And how long did the period of questioning and doubt go on? We have no idea. The songs of the early men were histories, of a kind. They sang of their times with the Clefts, and the cruelties were well recorded. There were songs that told of escape from pain and fear to this valley where the eagles were their friends, the deer gave them milk, and there were fish in the river and in the sea. They had shelter, better than the early heaps of sticks. They were brave and strong and healthy, and their numbers were growing . . . but they did not have the knack of giving life.

They were wild and restless, those first males, our so distant ancestors, and their nature took them long distances into the forests, and they began to know at least one part of their island, which was large, though they had no idea of that. They found great airy forests, deep and swift rivers and their tributaries, the little streams, pleasant hills, peaceful shores – this was what those earlier explorers found. They learned the ways of the wild animals and how to avoid them, and then, soon, how to kill them for food. They never killed the deer, their friends, whom they associated with gentleness and kindness, and with nourishment. They knew themselves to be better off, better fed, with much more space to move in, than the Clefts who never left their shore.

They were always tormented by the demands of their maleness, but did not know what it was they yearned for. All the tricks and devices for allaying sexual hunger were theirs, including the use of a certain animal – not a deer, they could not have brought themselves to use their milk donors, their mothers, in fact. But they did not use the words for mother, father. How could they? They did not know they were, or could be, fathers. And they were not deer, though they loved the deer. Did they know the word 'love', or think it? I believe not.

They thought often and with increasing urgency and curiosity about the Clefts, who lived exactly as they had always done, and not so far away. What had been an impossible distance for small boys was now nothing much. For the Clefts the walk to the Eagles' Hills was impossible because they had never thought of doing it. The idea of simply walking there, climbing, and seeing what was on the other side had never occurred to them. They did not know that on the other side of the mountain was the wonderful valley where the Monsters were living. It had never come into their heads to wonder. Out of sight, out of mind; and never has this been better exemplified.

Yet they were full of doubts now, and fearful. Their numbers were falling fast. They had never been very numerous, their instinctive inner regulator had seen to that. Some caves were half full, and then soon there were empty caves. Only half a dozen caves were occupied, and the old distinctions of Fish Catcher, Seaweed Gatherer and so on were blurring. The babies born Cleft were watched over, fretted over, were precious, while the Squirts were born to even stronger dislike, because it would have been better had they been born Clefts.

Two girls, young things, lying half in and half out of the waves on a favourite rock, watched as a certain sea creature inserted a tube into another of its kind, and emitted a cloud of milky eggs. They felt they had been granted a revelation – perhaps from the Great Fish himself – and they went to the Old Shes and told them what they had seen, and what they now thought likely to be the truth.

They were met by the slow tranquil gaze of eyes that had never been troubled by thought, even if they had learned anxiety, and no matter how these young Clefts persisted, saying that the Monsters might have a use, nothing would convince the old ones, if they had properly heard what was said.

Next time a Monster was born, these two snatched it away from the mother, and shielded it from the eagles, and examined the ugly thing that made it a Monster. They saw the tube was not unlike the one on the fish. Rubbed, it became stiff, but there was no emissions of cloudy eggs. The babe screamed, the eagle, waiting there behind a rock, rose up and broke its great wings into the girls' faces, and with its claws gently snatched the babe and carried it off. But it left behind questions and doubts.

So the two communities were thinking about each other, though the Clefts did not even dream of walking past the Killing Rock, to the mountain and over it.

As for the young lads, who were ranging further every day over their part of the island, fear of the Clefts kept them well away from those rocks and caves they had escaped from. Some did go up to the mountain where the eagles were, and stare towards the shore where they could see a rash of little pale splodges on the dark rocks – the Clefts, as usual lying half in, half out of the waves. But the boys did not go down that side of the mountain, they were too afraid.

Some did run along the rocky hills behind the shore where, if they persisted, they would reach the Clefts, but they did not persist, but always stopped where they could hide themselves, close enough to see what the females were doing. But they did not do much, only lazed and yawned, and swam a little and shook their long hair out over their shoulders to dry, and then swam again.

[The long hair is my invention, based on a mention of long hair from ages after this time. Perhaps the earliest Clefts were as smooth as seals, but then grew long hair in obedience to some imperative they were hardly conscious of. Historian]

The Clefts spent all day, days, many days in this way of doing nothing – as the boys saw it. They got tired of watching, but sometimes did go back, irresistibly pulled, their hungers pulling them, and one day saw a young Cleft walking alone by the waves not far from them. She stopped, turned her back on the watchers, and leaned her head back into her hands and stared out across the waves. This description of the girl, alone – the Clefts did not like being alone – taking her time to dawdle along the beach, hints that she was already one of the new Clefts where some kind of developmental yeast was brewing.

There were four boys (or Squirts) that day, on the higher rocks. An impulse took them and they crept down behind her, quiet, not really knowing what they intended to do. Then her nearness, and their hungers, defeated their fear of her and they ran forward and in a moment had her arms down by her sides, and were running her back towards their home valley. She let out short angry cries, her voice constricted by terror. She was not in the habit of panic, of alarm, and probably had never ever screamed or yelled. She was shocked into compliance. Taller than they were, much larger, but she was not stronger than four tough, well-muscled boys. They kept her running, while they cried out in triumph, which was fear, too. This was a Cleft they had there – and they had most thoroughly been taught fear of them. It was a good run from the part of the beach where they had found her, along the shoreline, then over the rocky hills to where the great river ran, before it burst in foam into the seas. Up the edge of this river they went, always running. She had begun to scream, roughly, in her unused voice. They stuffed handfuls of seaweed into her mouth.

Now, exhausted with running, half stifled with the weed, she moaned and gasped and then at last they were in the valley where the males lived. They were on the wrong side of the river. They swam her across it at a place where the waves ran less fiercely: that was no hardship to a girl who had swum and played in water since she was born. Then she was standing in the middle of a large group of Monsters, whom she had seen as babes, mutilated, or in the few moments between birth and being snatched away by the eagles. They were of all sizes, some children, some already past middle age, and these were the ones worst damaged, when they had been 'pets'. All of them naked, and seeing them there, the monsters, with their squirts pointed at her, she spat the weed out of her mouth and screamed, and this time it was a real scream, as if she had been doing it all her life.

One of her captors stuffed the weed back, and another tied her hands with strands of weed – all this clumsily and slowly, because this was the first time hands had been tied, and never had there been a captive, or prisoner.

And now instincts that had ranged free and untrammelled and often unrecognised spoke all at once in this crowd of males, and one of the captors threw down this soft, squirming female, and in a moment had his squirt inside her. In a moment he was off her and another had taken his place. The mass rape went on, it went on, they were feeding hungers it seemed they could never sate. Some lads who had gone off into the forest to find fruit came back, saw what was going on, and soon enough understood it and joined in. Then she no longer squirmed and kicked and moaned but lay still, and they understood, but not at once, that she was dead. And then, but not at once, that they had killed her. They dispersed then, not looking at each other, feeling shame, though they did not know what it was, and they left her there. The night was long and fearful and they were by now sickened by what had happened. If questions that had been tormenting them in some cases for years were being answered, by their flaccid squirts, their feelings of rest, relaxation and assuagement, they had killed, and they had never killed purposelessly.

In the morning light she lay there on the grass by

the river – dirty, smeared, smelling bad of their ex-
cretions, the wide empty eyes accusing them.

What were they to do?

Carry her to where the eagles would find her? But
something forbade them to do this.

In the end they carried her stiff soiled body to the
river bank where the water ran faster and pushed her
in, and watched her being swirled away downstream
towards the sea.

This was the first murder committed by our kind
(I except the exposing of crippled newborn infants)
and it taught them in that act what they were capable
of; they learned what their natures could be.

This murder was not recorded in their recitals of
their history and they tried to forget it, and in the
end did, just as the Clefts, when they did remember
how they had tortured and tormented the Squirts,
softened the tale and made it less, and then soon
chose to believe there had been one monstrous babe
they had hurt – just one.

We would not know about this murder if a very
old dying man had not become obsessed with his
memories, with this terrible day of rape and killing,
so long ago – he had been a boy – and he could
not stop repeating and repeating what he knew. Not
possible to ignore what he was saying, and some
young ones, hearing, shocked, distressed, preserved
the tale, which they could not forget, and in their

old age told it to the younger ones. This was, I believe, the beginning of the Squirts' oral annals, their Memories, at first coming into being almost by accident, but then valued and preserved. The female kept records – and I cannot bring myself to write down all that is there; and the male kept records: and I do bring myself to write down what is there.

Over among the Clefts, they noticed the absence of one of their own, wondered, fretted, in their soft lazy way, mentioned her absence, looked to see if she had fallen into one of the near pools, wondered again . . .

When the Squirts' distress had subsided, there remained a doubt which did not get less. Though the murdered girl had not been able to say much that was coherent, from the words she did say they knew that the language they used was poor compared with hers and, forced to worry over the question, find a reason, they at last understood that all they said had developed from the speech of small children who had made that first brave quest over the eagles' mountain. Their language was a child's, and it was even pitched high, like children's talk. Yes, they had new words, for the tools and utensils they had invented, but they talked together like children.

How were they to learn more, and better? Their dread of the Clefts, their fear of themselves and what they had done, made it impossible to go back to the shore, and find another Cleft and learn from her.

What were they to do?

It was a Cleft who did something. We do have to ask why it happened. After a period of time so long it is not possible to measure it, when no Cleft had had the curiosity to leave their maternal shore, one did just that. She walked towards the mountain where she knew the eagles took the Monsters, climbed the mountain, passed the eagles' nests, stood there on the height, and looked down and saw . . . we know what she saw, it is recorded.

Down there in the valley were a company of Monsters, moving about in activities she could not understand, or at the edge of the great river, and she had never seen a river, only the little rivulets that seeped down the cliffs. She was shocked into a fear that nearly took her running back to her shore. She could not see from where she stood the horrid bundles that made a Squirt what he was. They were at ease down there, those terrible creatures, and their voices floated up to her, talking as the Clefts did, but in high childish tones.

Why was she there at all? We do not know. Something in the stuff and substance of life had been agitated – by what? For ages – we use this dubious definition of time – no one had wanted to walk to the place that she could see down there . . . Just as not so very long ago the Clefts had – for no reason they could conjecture – begun to give birth to these Monsters, so now a Cleft was doing what not once one of them had done before: left her kind, driven by something that was no part of old Cleft nature.

She walked further, down the side of the mountain, and stopped. What were those strange pointed shapes down there? She thought at first they were alive, a kind of creature. They were the reed shelters the Squirts had evolved, a kind of reed that grew thick in the marsh that was the mouth of a river not far from here. The reeds were pale, and shone in the sunlight, and she saw that in their entrances sat Squirts, at their ease.

She made herself go forward, but slowly, but did not know how to signal that she did not mean harm. These were the creatures the Clefts had tormented and tortured and even mutilated. She herself had taken part in the work. They had seen her now, and were crowding together, facing her; she could see their faces turned upwards, staring, frightened.

She went on down.

Two enormous eagles were sitting apart from the crowding Squirts, and they were as tall as she was. Each was teasing at a great fish. As she watched, a boy came out of the river with a fish, which he deposited in front of the eagles, and he saw her and ran to his fellows.

51

They were not threatening her, but now they were smiling nervously, uncertain, as she was. She stood there in front of them, not knowing what to do, and they stood looking at her.

She was staring at their fronts, where the protuberances were. They did not seem so horrible now. She had seen baby Monsters, with their enormous swellings: out of proportion to the rest of them, as she realised.

She saw that some of the older ones were deformed, unlike the others, and did not at once know that these were the Cleft victims, grown and for ever disfigured.

A tree trunk had been dragged by them, or had fallen – and her tiredness, for it had been a long way for a Cleft, made her subside on it to rest. As she sat there, slowly they came crowding up, staring, and it was at her middle, which was naked, because this was halfway between full moon and full moon, and no blood flowed then.

She could see everything of their differences from her; they could see little of hers from them.

One, grown, sat by her on the trunk, staring always at her face, her breasts, the large loose lolling breasts, at her middle. Driven as she was, she put out a hand to touch his protuberance, the terrifying thing that for all her life had been horrible to her, and at once it rose up into her hand and she felt it throb and pulse. What had driven her here was an imperative, and in a moment she and this alien were together, and his tube was inside her and behaved as its name suggested.

They stared at each other, serious – and separated.

They resumed sitting near each other, looking. She curiously handled his new flaccid tube; and he was feeling and probing her.

Parents interested enough in their children's development to drop in on nursery games will be able to say what was happening now: they will have seen it all.

Naked, because of an imminent bath, or change of clothes, the two little children are standing looking at each other. This is not of course the first time brother and sister have seen each other nude, but for some reason both have been alerted to the other's differences.

'Why have you got that *thing*,' somewhat petulantly enquires the girl – but we have to imagine that what the tones of their voices suggest refers to far in the future adulthood.

'Because I am a boy,' announces the child, and what he is saying dictates a whole series of postures. He thrusts out his pelvis, and makes some jerky movements which he seems to associate with some game. He holds the tip of his penis down and releases it in a springing gesture. All the time he frowns belligerently, not at his sister, but probably at some imaginary male antagonist.

The little girl, seeing all these achievements, none of which are possible to her, frowns, looks down at her centre and says, 'But I am nicer than you.'

The boy, frowning at her cleft, which no one could say is threatening or even assertive, now adds to his repertoire of cocky tricks with some others, rolling his balls about in their sac.

'I like me much better than I like you,' says the little girl, but she approaches her brother and says, 'Let me feel.'

He shuts his eyes, holds his breath, endures her pulling and rolling, and says, 'Now, let me feel you.'

At which he inexpertly probes the crevices and announces, 'Your pee-thing is not as nice as my pee-thing.'

'My pee-thing is better than your pee-thing,' she insists.

There are two slave girls in the room, their nurses. They have been watching this play (foreplay) with knowing worldly smiles, which relate to one's husband and the other's lover.

At the little boy's thrusting and showing off, they exchange what-do-you-expect-from-a-male smiles, and both show signs of wanting to shield the girl, who after all has a hymen to protect.

One says, 'Your mother'll be cross if she sees you,' making a ritual close to the play.

They do not immediately separate but the boy

gives a little tug at the girl's hair and then kisses her shyly on the cheek. She, for her part, gives him a hug. The slave girls put on appropriate smiles, oh-what-dear-little-things.

This particular little play is for now, the girl about five, the boy a little younger. The children wouldn't want to repeat it, let's say, next year.

She will be into maternal and nurturing games, he already a legionnaire – a soldier.

You may be thinking that I write of these scenes with too much assurance? But I feel more certainly about them than about many I have attempted to describe. And now I must explain why by way of what may seem a diversion, even an irrelevance.

I married young a girl approved by my parents, and we had two children – boys. I was ambitious, planning to become a senator, worked hard, cultivated the suitable connections, and had very little time for my wife and less for my boys. She was an admirable mother; they had for me a distant regard. I did everything I could for them in the way of easing their way into the army, where they did well. But both were killed fighting against the German tribes. When they were dead I regretted how little I had known these young men whom everyone commended. I think it is not uncommon for a man in his second marriage to regret what he had omitted in his first. I thought a good deal about my two sons when this could do no good to them at all. My first wife died. I lived alone for years. I became ill and took a long time to recover. Friends came to see me, and I was recommended to marry again. I thought of my first wife and knew that we could have loved each other, if I had had the time for it.

When I was convalescing, a girl from a junior branch of the family, Julia, arrived to look after me. I knew what was happening: the mother had of course hoped that her well-off relative would 'do something' for her, her children. But there were so many of them. I had observed that if a man takes an interest in one member of a too abundant family, it will not be long before he is taking on the whole tribe. Julia was pleasant, pretty, attentive, and did not talk about her needy sisters and brothers. I enjoyed her, her genuine simplicity, the fresh observations of a clever little provincial girl, who watched everything that went on, so as to model herself on the ways of the elite. I am sure I can truthfully say she liked me, though I was always aware – and made myself remain wary – that an old man should not expect too much of a very attractive woman a third his age. Young relatives and young men who thought of me as a patron were suddenly often in my house, and I thought it would not be long before she married one of them, causing me a little pang or two: and this was – contradictorily – because I thought so much of my first wife and what I had missed. And those boys, those wonderful young men, whose childhood I had scarcely been conscious of.

I asked Julia to marry me, saying that we must agree on a deal. She would give me two children, and I would ask nothing of her beyond that, and she and the children would be well provided for. She agreed, but not without hesitation, having learned that young men were desiring her in plenty. But they weren't rich, like me. And she did like me, as a friend. Or perhaps as a tutor? She told me she enjoyed talking with me and listening to me because 'I learn such a lot, you see'. She was almost completely ignorant.

And now something unexpected. I had taken it for granted that this fresh, plump girl ('my little partridge') would bring forth children easily, but her first pregnancy was difficult and the birth worse. She told me it was because she had bad illnesses as a child, and sometimes the family didn't get enough to eat. If she had asked me to let her renege on the second half of our bargain – the second child – I would have been ready to forgive her. I had not enjoyed seeing her discomfort, and then the difficult birth. But she was an honest girl, the partridge, and she went ahead for the second child, though she had a bad enough time with that one, too.

The two infants once born were handed into the care of the slave girls working in the children's wing – and I don't think she thereafter ever thought of them. It had not occurred to me to make part of our bargain 'Give me two babes and be a mother to them'. But when I did tax her about her indifference to her children she said, 'Bad enough having to be a child without having to look after them too.' I learned that she was the eldest of the children, with a sickly and worn-out mother, and she had had to be a mother to her siblings, with the help of one inadequate slave girl, a runaway slave from some great estate, where they treated slaves badly. Julia's helper could hardly speak our language – she was Greek. Julia had sworn that when she got to maturity she would refuse to marry a man who could not provide her with slaves. A pretty big oath to swear, if you are very poor, from a small country town. But that explained why she agreed with her mother to come and offer her services to me.

Her delay in agreeing to 'make a deal' with me was explained. I could not have asked her to do anything more difficult than to have a child, let alone two.

She said, too, that she did not have motherly feelings, she never had them. She had asked her mother why she was always ordered to feed and wash the babies but her brothers were not. Her mother simply said that this was how things were. It is not recorded what the Greek slave thought about it all, but no one would be interested in her.

Julia's uninhibited remarks were thought most original and daring, but she did not understand why people laughed at them and commended her. At first I am sure she did not intend to shock or surprise, though she was acquiring a reputation for her wit and boldness. Soon she was in circles whose prevailing tone was a world-weary cynicism, and then she did play up to it: what had been fresh and natural to her became a style; she fitted in with people I didn't like, and there was not much left in her of the small-town girl with her own view on life.

I did say to her that her generation struck people of mine as selfish, self-indulgent, amoral, compared with the women like my mother, who were virtuous and famed for their piety and strength of character. Julia seemed interested in my strictures, but as if they could have nothing at all to do with her; as if I had said, 'Did you know that in Britain there are tribes who paint themselves blue?' 'Fancy that,' she could have said, as a cloud of doubt crossed her face. But she knew I did tell her the truth, so decided to believe me. 'Blue, eh? They must look funny, then.' Her characteristic expression was open and frank, and she smiled her appreciation of this brave new world. When, soon, she became notorious for her immorality, her self-indulgence, like all the women of her circle, I would imagine her, with her honest face, her look of friendly interest in everything, hearing from some fellow accomplice in an orgy that now she must try this or that, saying, 'Oh, really? People do this, do they? Well, fancy that. Let's have a go.'

If Julia never went near the nursery wing, I could hardly be got away from it. I have never been more intrigued, not even by some great affair of state.

Even when the babes were infants, I found plenty to astonish me and when they became three, four, five, every day was a revelation. I never interfered with the management by the nursery slaves, took no part unless some little thing came up for an embrace or to be noticed. I heard one girl say to the other, 'They don't have a mother, but their grandfather makes up for it.'

While I was being daily amazed by what I was observing, the thick package of the history of the Clefts and Monsters, of the very early birth of the male from the female, was given to me by a scholar who had before suggested I might tackle this or that topic. I had had things published, had been noticed, but never under my own name – which might astonish you, did you hear it. This enterprise quite simply frightened me. First, the material, ancient scrolls and fragments of scrolls, loose and disordered scraps of paper, in the old scripts that were the first receptacles of the transfer of 'the mouth to ear' mode of the first histories. A great pack of the stuff, and while there was some kind of order in it, it was not necessarily how I would have arranged it. Every time I took it up to consider my place in the story I was dismayed, not only by the scale of the task but because this tale was so far from me that I did not know how to interpret it.

And then I watched, in the nursery, this little scene. The girl, Lydia, was about four, the boy younger, perhaps two. Lydia must have observed a hundred times the protuberances in front of her brother, Titus, but on this day she stared at him and said, 'What's that you've got there?' Her face! She was intrigued, shocked, envious, repelled – she was gripped by strong contradictory emotions. I watched, and so did the slave girls. We knew that this was a momentous event.

At this Titus pushed forward his equipment, and began

wagging his penis up and down, looking at her with lordly air. 'It's mine, it's mine,' he chanted and said, 'And what have you got? You haven't got anything.'

Lydia was standing looking down at her smooth front with the little pink cleft. 'Why?' she demanded of the girls, of me, of her brother. 'Why have you got that, and I haven't?'

'It's because you are a girl,' says the little lord and master. 'I am a boy and you are a girl.'

'I think it's ugly, you are horrible,' she states, comes nearer to him, and says, 'I want it.'

He swings his hips about, evading her probing hand, singing, 'You can't, you can't, and so that's *that*.'

'I want to touch,' she demands, and this time he leaves his protuberances just within reach, but withdraws them suddenly as her hand approaches.

'Then I won't let you look at mine,' she says and turns herself round, hiding herself.

At which he sings, 'I don't care, why should I care, you're just *silly*.'

'I'm *not* silly,' she half screams, and runs to the girls. 'Why, why, why?' she demands, as one whisks her up in her arms.

'Don't cry,' says this nurse. 'Don't give him that satisfaction.'

'It's not fair,' sobs the child, and the other girl says, 'But if you had that you wouldn't know what to do with it,' sending me a great wink, and a laugh. (But I have never been that kind of Master: perhaps she wished I were.)

And at that moment I knew I would at least try and take on this task, my history of that ancient, long-ago time. Scenes I had pondered over, thinking, but after these ages, how can you really understand what it meant when females and the males were together in that valley, while the eagles watched them, not knowing anything – and we Romans know so much – about why the girls were shaped like this, and the boys like that, let alone what it all meant.

They were driven by powerful instincts – and we do know how strong they are, nothing has changed there – but I keep coming back to a thought: that the boys seemed to be hungering for something, wanting something, needing – but did not know what it was their squirts wanted – forcing all the rest of themselves to want, to need.

And the girls: organs they did not know they had drove them across the mountain to the boys, and even when they knew that mating meant later births, they did not know why. Or for a long time they didn't.

It was because of my observations in the nursery wing that I decided to attempt this history, despite the difficulties. I am sure that certain exchanges between the males and the females would not have altered all that much, in spite of the long ages (and ages – etc.). That scene I saw in the nursery was enacted then, or something like it. Must have been.

And how about the scene I saw when the boy Titus, waking in the morning with an erection, slowly stood up, grasping the sides of his bed, looking down, and shouting, 'Mine! It's mine! Mine, mine, mine, mine . . .'

So much I believe has not changed. But if those old people could come back, and observe, and see, and find so much unchanged, then other things they would not understand at all.

My account of my marriage, my Julia, my first and second families, they would not recognise. The old senator and his young wife? No. Why not? A very simple reason: they did not live long. It was a hard and dangerous time and not even the 'Old Shes', the 'Old Ones', could have been very old. An 'old female' we hear and what do we see? Some grey-haired, wrinkled, bent old crone. Nothing in any of the records describes an aged person.

No one I have ever met, or have heard of, would *not* at once understand 'The old senator and his very young wife'. They might smile, or grimace, or look condemning, but they would know what is involved here. And so I begin this history, this present history, even when I was daily in the nursery, watching the children, and while Julia was off, mostly with her new friends.

She never lied to me, except by omission. It was assumed she had a lover, and she encouraged me to think that. What need did I have of more information when the material was at my disposal of Rome's secret services? She was now an intimate of some very highly placed circles: parties that can only be called orgies went on every night. She was friends with infamous women, and with others who did not survive into the next emperor's reign.

I did say to her, when she was sitting there after some great party or other, watching me, as if she expected me to reprimand her, 'Julia, you are flying too high.' I waited for her to defend herself but she didn't. Perhaps she was herself troubled. 'The higher you fly the further you fall,' I said, smiling, so as not to seem judgemental. 'Be careful, Julia.'

And she was, for she is still alive.

And the two lovely children, who I can say truthfully have been the best blessings of my life?

The girl, Lydia, is now much with her mother. How could she not have admired the elegant woman, so beautiful, that Julia had evolved into? Lydia goes to parties and – I don't know how much worse – with her mother. She announces she intends to make a great marriage. The boy is energetic, brave, full of manly games and feats and endurances – and everything we would expect of a Roman boy at his best. He wants to go into the army. He thinks perhaps he could be one of the Praetorian Guards. And why not? The Guard is made up of handsome young men like him.

It occurs to me that perhaps it may be said of me, 'He gave three of his sons to die for the empire, he was a true Roman.' It will probably not be remembered that once I fancied myself as a serious historian.

The others stood around, staring. She saw that as they leaned and stared, restrained by knowing how they had hurt the other girl, their tubes were all pointing at her, like a question. She wanted to get away; wanted to do what was natural to her, which was to slide into water and lose herself in it. She got up, conscious all the time that what she did was provoking the boys, and went to the banks of the river, where they had made a little bay and the water was shallow. She knelt in it and splashed, though this cold water was not like the balmy sea water she was used to. When she rose from the water and faced them, crowding there after her, she saw one of the great shell containers they had made. She picked one up, and they told her its name. They had made knives of the sharp shells: she learned that word too. They kept at her, saying sentences and words in that childish speech of theirs, while she replied to them, and they copied what she said, not for its sense but its sound.

Meanwhile, the two eagles had finished their meal and lifted off on those great wings, and gone back up to the mountain. The sun was going down. She was afraid, alone in this strange place, with these strangers . . . *People* was the word the Clefts used for themselves, but these must be people too, for every one had been born to a Cleft. She might herself have given birth to one of these staring Monsters . . . she knew she had made a Monster, snatched away from her as it appeared, put out to die, taken away by the great birds.

But they didn't die. None of them had died. Here

they all were, and like Clefts, except for those flat chests where nipples appeared, uselessly, and the bundles of tubes and balls there in front.

A shadow was creeping towards them from the mountain. She was becoming afraid, and she had not been until now. They were still crowding around her, and the need and hunger for her was so evident that again she did as some need inside her she knew nothing about was telling her. One after another she held those stiff tubes in her hand until they emptied themselves, and then just as she had been brought here by a need, now she had to leave . . . had to, and followed by them all, she walked towards the mountain. She did not run. Running was not what Clefts did. But it was a fast walk, propelled by fear. Of what? The Monsters – so close? The night – so near? She reached the foot of the mountain as dark came and it was a heavy dark, without a helping moon. She found what she needed, a cave, and there she sheltered. She did not sleep. Her mind was too full of thoughts, all new to her. Very early, in the dawn light, she left the cave, and saw that down in the valley no people were visible. They were inside those shelters they made of shining river reed.

As fast as she could, up the mountain she went, this girl who had scarcely taken more than a few steps together in her life, and to the top and past the great eagles, motionless and asleep on their tall rocks, and down the other side, and reached the shore where her people were, lying about as they always were, singing a little, spreading out their long hair. They had scarcely noticed she had been away.

The Old Shes were all together on a big flat rock, their place. She saw as if for the first time those vast loose laps and dewlaps of flesh, enormous loose breasts, the big slack faces with eyes that seemed to see nothing, bodies half in, half out of the warm waves. She saw it all and disliked what she saw.

She had to tell them what had happened, and it was not that they didn't listen, they didn't seem able to take in what she said. Over the mountain were living the Monsters they had put out to die – that was the very first fact, and she might as well not have spoken at all. The younger Clefts were almost as bad, except a girl, one of those who had tried to tell the Old Shes about the Monsters' tubes, did hear her and wanted to know everything. These two girls were always together now, talking, speculating. In due time a babe was born – a Cleft. She knew and her friend knew that this babe was different, and they looked for signs of the difference. Nothing to see, but it was a restless, crying babe and it crawled and swam and then walked early.

This first babe born to the Clefts, with a Monster for a father, was, these two girls knew, different in its deepest nature. But saying this poses a question, does it not? How did they know? What was so different in them that made it possible for them to know? Something had happened to these two Clefts, but they did not know what it was. All they knew was that when they talked together about the new babe, about the Monsters over the mountain, they were using language and ideas they could not share with anyone else on that shore.

The girl who had gone over the mountain, because she had been forced to by a new inner nature, was one of the Water Carers. She saw to it that the trickles of water that come down the cliffs were kept clean, and directed into a rocky pool made for that purpose. She was known as Water, but one day, summoned by the Old Shes for some task or other, she said, not having thought or planned it, 'My name is Maire.' Which is what they called the half moon, before it became full moon. Her friend, the other girl, who was one of the Fish Catchers and, therefore, Fish, said, 'And my name is Astre.' Which is what they called the brightest star at evening.

The Old Shes seemed annoyed, if they had actually heard what the girls said. As long as the young Clefts tended them and gave them food, they could call themselves what they liked – this was what the girls suspected was felt.

This kind of critical thought about the Old Shes

was new: so many new dangerous thoughts in their heads.

Maire thought a good deal about the Squirts over the mountain. She *felt* them as wanting her. It was not how she had handled their squirts that was in her mind: rather the hunger in their faces as they looked at her, a need that was like something pulling at her.

The new people in their valley thought of Maire. They had no memories of the very first Cleft they had killed, but they remembered Maire, and with longing. Sometimes they crept along the rocky hills above the old shore to catch a glimpse of the Clefts, but were afraid of being seen by them. All their thoughts of the Clefts were dark and troubling. The Clefts had the gift of making new people: they, the newest people, did not.

And then they were more and more troubled by their speech. The Clefts' speech was clearer and better. They tried to remember words used by Maire, and how she put them together. But they didn't know enough, they knew so little.

Perhaps she would come again?

Meanwhile, the eagles were not bringing them any new babies. This was because none had been born.

Next, Astre gave birth. It was a baby Monster and she and Maire, without talking about it, or planning, decided to take the babe over the mountain themselves.

The eagles were waiting as always on the Killing Rock but Astre wrapped the new babe in seaweed and Maire left her own new child, a Cleft, to be cared for by the others.

The two girls walked towards the mountain, slowly because Astre had recently given birth. An eagle was with them, flying just above their heads, and with its eyes always on the bundle in Astre's arms. The great wings were balanced there so as to make shadow that kept them shielded from the sun. Was this deliberate? It certainly seemed that the eagle was trying to protect them, or the baby. When they reached the mountain, the two sat down to rest while Astre fed the baby. This was the first and last time this babe was given its mother's milk. The eagle settled near, closing its wings with a slide of feathers on sleek feathers: the air reached them like a puff of cool wind.

Then, rested, Astre was ready to climb, and up they went, the eagle always just above them, to the top. There Maire put her arm round Astre, knowing what a shock it was, seeing the populated valley for the first time.

It was after midday. The tall slanting reed huts sent hard shadows across the grass to where the boys were at their various tasks. One of them saw the girls, shouted, and they all ran to where they could watch them descend. Down, down, they went, through the sharp rocks, the eagle always overhead.

When they had reached the level ground, the boys came crowding forward and as Maire remembered, their hungry need was in their eyes like a plea. Astre held the babe tight to her, and tried to smile as she walked forward, though she was trembling, and held tight to Maire. All around her now were the monstrous boys with their knotty bundles there in front of them. The babe was beginning to cry, inside its wraps of weeds. Astre threw away the weed and held out the baby for them all to see. This was why she and Maire had come, with the babe, but now she was about to say goodbye to it she felt bereft and alone. She did not remember before feeling this, though she had once given birth to a Monster, which had been put out on the Rock. One of these lads there, in front of her, could have been that abandoned babe. A lad came forward to take the baby, and Astre let it go. She was beginning to weep.

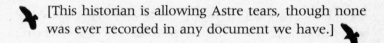

[This historian is allowing Astre tears, though none was ever recorded in any document we have.]

Because the baby was crying, milk ran from her breasts and she shielded them with her arms, feeling for the first time a need for concealment.

The lad with the baby went to the edge of the

forest and whistled. Now the baby was crying loudly. Soon a doe appeared, flicking her tail, and stood looking at them out of the trees. The lad went forward with the baby and laid it on the ground. The doe came and lay down near the babe. The doe licked the baby. He, for his part, did not know what to do. Astre, watching, cried even harder, seeing the doe's tenderness. The lad gently knelt by the couple, doe and baby, and pushed the babe's face close to the doe's teats. Still the babe cried – and then stopped. He was suckling while the doe licked and licked. The tiny hands were clutching at the doe's fur, and it was that which made Astre sink on to the great tree trunk and put her head in her hands. Maire sat by her, and held her. The babe suckled and was pleased, waving its little arms about, and the doe seemed pleased too. Then she rose, leaving the babe, and went to eat grass nearby.

The lad who had cared for the babe's need sat by Astre on the trunk and put his arm clumsily round her. It was noticeable that his delicacy with the baby was not repeated when he tried to caress Astre. Maire, seeing that Astre was well-supported, got up, touched one of the youths on his shoulder to turn him to her, and then held his squirt. The two copulated, standing. In the course of that afternoon and evening Maire copulated with them all. What I think we must imagine here is the flickering fast coupling of birds, which we all may see when we go to our farms and estates as the warm weather comes.

Astre watched, her arms folded across her chest. She shook her head when one of the Squirts seemed to invite her to do as Maire was doing. She was bleeding still, after giving birth, and soon went to the river to see if there was riverweed she could use. Yes, there was, nothing like the seaweed the Clefts used, and she made herself a bandage. The boys watched, and when they saw the blood running seemed to understand.

The doe again fed the baby and then went off into the forest, while the baby cried. *Crying for its mother*: so Astre understood, and did not know if she was weeping for herself or for all the little babies (who were probably here, all around her) once left without mothers, or even mothers' milk.

At evening the great eagle, who had been watching all this with its yellow eyes, took off back up to his nest at the top of the mountain.

It was warm, a mild night. The girls were fed fish from the river, and river water from the big shells. They lay near the tree trunk and watched while the community of lads (and some older ones, mutilated badly, though the girls could not judge this) went into the reed shelters for the night, which shone brightly in the moonlight, frightening both girls, though Maire had seen the shelters before. They slept, close by each other. In the night lads came from the shelters to see if the girls were still there, and because of their caution, looking into the trees, looking around, the girls understood the shelters were for a purpose.

And the doe? The babe? They were there, hidden in bushes. And if some wild animal did come down from the trees, these two creatures would not have much hope of survival.

When the girls woke, everyone was out of the shelters, now shining in sunlight, and the babe was lying near the doe who was lying down and stretched out to feed it. Again fish and water were brought to the girls, and – what they had scarcely tasted before – fruit from the forest.

We have accounts of the visit of the two girls, Maire and Astre, from the male records – ours – and from the Clefts' histories. They do not disagree, and both insist that what the boys wanted now were lessons how to speak. Listening to the Clefts, they had learned of their clumsiness.

Both sides were learning fast from the other, particularly as the more they learned, the more they knew how much there was for them to know.

The girls looked inside the shelters and found a filthy mess of bones, fruit rinds, discarded weed bandages. They tore branches from the trees and used them as brooms. This was in itself remarkable since there were no trees near the Clefts' shore. The rubbish was swept into a big pile and added to it were the bones and bits of flesh from the place where fish was brought to the eagles. This pile was swept to the river's edge, then into the cleansing flow.

The males caught fish, cut it up with knives made from shells, looked for fruit in the trees, made sure the girls, and the baby when it cried, were fed. They brought fresh grass for the doe, and petted the doe and the baby.

The girls watched everything, just as the boys watched them. They copulated all the time, as if this was what the girls had come for. Astre too, as her birth flow stopped.

Astre and Maire sat on the log, with the boys around them, and they spoke sentences, slowly, carefully, easy to hear and repeat. It was already evident that two languages were developing, one being learned from these new arrivals, and one high and childish, which was how the very first community of boys had to speak. They spoke like children, even as little children, and how they did dislike what they heard from each other. Maire and Astre had to be there, to teach them language, teach them how to keep their shelters clean – and to mate with them when their tubes grew alert and pointed at the girls.

In the records nothing much is made of this continual copulation, much more of how the young males tried to be close to the girls, nuzzling and hugging and even licking them, as they had watched the doe licking the babies – which was what their experience of mother love had been. All had been licked and nuzzled by the kindly does. None had ever been loved by a mother. They were hungry for touch and tenderness; and the girls, who on their own shore did not go in much for this kind of affection, were surprised and pleased.

Apart from these scenes of . . . yes, let us call it love, were the very early Monsters, who had been badly hurt by the Clefts. They feared the females, and tried to keep away from them. The girls feared them, because of the emotions they felt. Shame? All they knew was that the hot dark stares of these damaged males, who might very well have been their own offspring, made them feel as if they were ill.

And then, one morning, the two girls simply left. The same inner compulsion that had brought them here now took them away over the mountain and to their own shore.

Their time for conception had come and gone – though of course they had no idea of that. This rider is often seen in our records: the males' not the Clefts'. But when we say things like that now, 'they did not know', 'they were so primitive', 'they were too ignorant' – the gamut of dismissing phrases – well I, for one, wonder. How do we know what they knew, and how?

So long ago it was, even if we do not know how long. 'Ages' – it will do. Ages ago, these primitive people, our ancestors, whose thoughts still live in us – we have their thoughts once spoken, now written – ages and ages ago they did this and they did that but never knew why. So we like to think now.

We have a need to describe creatures other than us as stupid or at least as unthinking.

The girls did not leave unnoticed. The young men stared after them, and if the girls had turned round the faces full of longing would have told them everything.

Then the youths ran to the top of the mountain and watched how the girls went down the other side, past the Killing Rock – and then reached their shore.

They had gone!

When would they come again? *When*, oh when?

Two young women stood at the top of a rock they had climbed so they could look down on their shore . . . their home . . . their people. They were Clefts . . . well, of course, but although they had been in the valley with the people they once called Monsters, their minds must have been full of like, unlike; same, other; – full of differences. Did they think of themselves as female, and other than male? Young females. They were not old, they were not Old Shes. They were of the people, at whom they were staring, impelled to do this because – precisely

– their minds were full of differences. Without males, or Monsters, no need ever to think that they were Clefts; without the opposite, no need to claim what they were. When the first baby Monster was born, Male and Female was born too, because before that were simply, the people.

Two young females stood on their rock and looked at the seashore where lolled their kin – themselves. But in those eyes of theirs (I shall make them blue because of the blue sky and blue seas that surrounded them) once so calm and unreflecting were shadows and, precisely, shadows of the young males they had just left (possibly their sons, but who knew?). Young males, but surely the people, just like the people they were looking at. How else, if the Monsters had been born of the people here, those bodies lolling about on the rocks.

Monsters . . . these two had once thought like that because there was nothing else to think.

They stood looking, contrasting what they saw with the vigour and movement of the valley over the mountain. How slow and quiet that scene down there. There was one place of movement and noise, which sounded like a protest. The babe that Maire had borne not very long before . . . and here was another new thought. How long ago had she given birth to that babe over there, who was, and there could be no doubt about that, half-Monster, even if she was a Cleft? What need had there ever been to define time? It was such a time ago, we did this then . . . when . . . but everybody knew the times of the moon, sometimes large and round, or like a slice of pale fingernail, with sizes between. Everyone knew the correspondence between the red flood that matched the red flow from The Cleft, and the moon being fat and bright and close. But *when* had that babe been born, because it was clear there was a correspondence between that and its relation with the Monsters (or people) over there in the valley.

A slow sleepy scene, with one agitated babe, Maire's child, and the two could see that the Cleft who held the child was annoyed and impatient. Babies did not complain and agitate and become nuisances and flail about. Who behaved like that, all movement and energy, if not a Squirt?

The babe's minder was sitting on a rock at the very edge of the waves, and it would be easy to let a little thing like that slide into a wave and be lost. Who would notice? If anyone did, the move to save it would be slow and lazy. Lazy and languid . . . and into the minds of the two females, for they were that whether they knew it or not, or felt no need to think it, came a surely new emotion. It was disgust. No, not new, for disgust was what used to be felt when they saw a newborn Monster, with his ugly parts. No, disgust was not new, but to feel it when looking at the old females, the Old Shes, yes, that was new.

Immediately in front of the two girls was a large, flat, comfortable rock where the old Clefts lolled by the right of long use. Large, flabby Clefts, their flesh all about them in layers of fat – there they lay with their legs sprawled, and their clefts were fatty and full, with pale hair growing over tongues and pulps of pinkish flesh. Ugly, oh so ugly, thought these girls who had shuddered at the little Monsters' pipes and bulges.

And the general look of them . . . at the same moment into the minds of the two came the idea of sea slugs – there they were in the sea now. It was as if water had chosen to be enclosed by skins of jellified water, large loose shapes, that were not shapes, since they changed and with every wave and inside these sacs of transparent skin were the faint outlines of organs, of tubes and lumps of working matter. And each vast shapeless Thing had two little eyes, just like the tiny eyes of the old Clefts there, lost in the loose flesh of their faces, old Clefts sprawling and dozing on the warm rocks, and the thought in both girls' minds now, and perhaps it was the first time it had ever been thought in that long-ago time such ages ago, came: 'I don't want to be like them' . . . the idea that had made revolutions, wars, split families, or driven the bearer of the idea mad or into new active life . . . 'I won't be like them, I *won't*.' Maire and Astre were shuddering at the horror of what they saw, horror of what they might become. And all the while the sea shushed and lolled about and lazed, murmuring its sibilants, and it was not, could never be, still, unless it whipped itself into a storm. The sound of the loving lazing sea, which had been in their ears always, all their lives, but over the mountain where the sea shores were a good way off the sound was absent. The wind beating about in the trees, yes, or the cry of the eagles, the splash of a great fish in the river, which rushed past, but never this enervating lulling, lapsing and whispering . . . the babe was trying to stand in the nurse's arms. But it was not old enough yet to want to stand . . . what sort of a thought was that? Babes nursed and bottoms leaked, and they grew and they crawled and you had to watch them, or they crawled into the waves . . . some did, some always had . . . and then they walked and ran and were Clefts, smaller than the big Clefts but just like them. But they did not strive and try to stand so very young.

Maire reached for her babe just as the impatient nurse was about to drop it on the crest of a wave.

The nurse said, 'Yes, take it, take it away. What kind of a child is that?' And went off to sulk her annoyances with the others of her kind – that is, the youngest of those Clefts who were not children.

The babe in Maire's arms was very strong. She could hardly hold it.

Because Maire was pregnant, she had milk: the Clefts' breasts were usually full of milk. They suckled any babe around that needed it, there was not then such a feeling of *mine*, or *not mine*, among these ancient people. The fierceness of *mine* – well, it had to come in from somewhere, since its existence is evident, and as far as we know has always been with us. Always? Those long-ago people, the first people, the Clefts, did not think, or not so much, Mine, Yours. Or so I believe.

The two girls sat among their kind, among their kin, as always, and the others looked at them, including the Old Ones, who lay about like stranded sea slugs. Their eyes, when they did focus on the girls, were hostile.

That night the two went to one of the empty caves, as if they had discussed and planned it. They could not share a cave with the others: and there was no reason to. There were plenty of empty caves, their possible inhabitants were over the mountain in the valley. This cave was on the edge of the cliff and looked directly down at the shore. From its opening could be seen the mouths of other caves. They could defend themselves well here. And what a sad thought that was, when nothing like it had been in their minds before.

Two young women, both pregnant, and Maire's first baby got from the young men: the first baby ever of the new kind, who had so nearly been allowed to drift away on the crest of a big wave.

When the two were well swollen with the new pregnancies, they both went to the Old Ones, the Shes, and told them that these new babes, when born, would be half-Monsters, just like Maire's first, called the New One. But the suspicious old eyes stared and peered, the old faces seemed to shiver in revulsion – but nothing was said.

The next thing that happened was sudden and violent. Two of the young Clefts gave birth, to Monsters, at the same time. They were on the rocks near to the sea. The Old Clefts called to them to throw the new babes into the sea, but at once Astre and Maire were there, just as the babies were being cut free from their mothers, who were shouting their repulsion and their fear of their infants. Maire, her own New One in one arm, held a new baby Monster in the other; Astre snatched up a babe, and the two went as fast as they could – remember that running was not something they were used to – to the Killing Rock. Two eagles were floating down from their mountain. Some of the young Clefts came crowding up from their shore, to watch how the eagles took off with the new Monsters.

Astre and Maire stood there on the edge of the Killing Rock, calm and self-possessed, though they were in danger.

And now the two girls began telling the young Clefts about the grown Monsters who lived over there, beyond the mountain. They were people, just like us, said Maire and Astre, speaking slowly because these ideas were difficult and hard to take in. They were people except that in front of their bodies they had the tubes and lumps that made new babes. That was what they were for. So said Maire, so said Astre, standing there before the others facing their hostile looks, their threatening faces.

Now the two spent their time in the entrance to their great cave, their airy cave with its clean sandy floor and walls sparkling with the crystalline rocks of the region. It was full of sunlight when the sun was setting: these caves faced west: a word, an idea, which would not be known to these people – to us – for . . . well, I may say thousands of years and no one will contradict me.

They were there, instead of inside the cave's deep coolness, because they could watch what went on down on the shore, their shore. It had been their shore but now they were afraid. The two girls, both so pregnant, and the infant, the New One, were visible to anyone choosing to glance up, and the glances were hostile. Down there, the girls knew, those Clefts were their kin, like them, their kind – and were too indolent to keep a regular watch on what they feared: Maire, and Astre. The laziness of their sisters meant that Maire and Astre were safe from them. Sisters: those Clefts down there were not merely kin, but sisters. You may have sisters even without brothers, though already the word 'sisters' had within it a sense of something in opposition.

What a sleepy indolent scene, down there on the

rocks. The Clefts might lie dozing from one high tide until the next splashed their feet with chilly water. Then they yawned, slid into the waves, swam a little, climbed back to loll on the rocks.

Above them was the mouth of the cave where the difficult sisters Astre and Maire sat, dandling the infant, the New One. They cradled and soothed this child more than either had ever done with a child; but earlier babes had not cried and fretted and this one did. They tried to hush the infant, not wanting to alert the attention of their sisters down there. But still the baby cried, and it was a sound that gritted on those placid lazy nerves, so unused to feeling irritated or annoyed. Why did she cry so much, this very first member of the race to come, our race, the human race – though the two had not got as far as *that* thought while suspecting that something new was here, with the New One.

What was this new Cleft, that had in her the substance of the Monsters? Babies did not cry unless they were hungry or wanted to be dipped into the waves, or even allowed to swim a little – these people might swim before they walked, so at home were they in the water. Babies did not as a rule cry. But this one might sob or even wail as if its little heart were broken. Was she, this new type of Cleft, new Person, aware of her strange new nature? It sounded like grief, the weeping she did; but grief was not something these people went in for. They did not love each other with intensity and exclusiveness, they did not say, 'I want only her, that one'; did not desire to hear, 'I want only that one.'

Without the 'only that one', without wanting and craving the Other, and only the Other, some kinds of grief did not arise.

But this babe sounded desolate, lacking something. And the two girls, because of the babe's crying, felt a new emotion because of the New One.

Ideas, emotions, words, thoughts, that have been inhabiting the minds of us, the human race, quite comfortably and at least without strain, were presenting themselves now to these young Clefts, and they were restless and disturbed, sitting there at the mouth of their cave.

The three of them, the two females and their babe, soon to be five with the two soon to be born, were something new in this world of ours, a new thing, and they could have been swept out of existence by a fall of rock, or an enemy creeping up on them . . . an *enemy*? What was that? An enemy is someone who wants to harm you. Those Clefts down there, dozing on their rocks, and the Old Ones particularly, were enemies.

At night, in the dark, when the moon was absent, they went to the back of the very long cave, and positioned themselves behind outcrops of rocks, different ones every night. It would be so easy for someone to come creeping in, unseen when not outlined against

the stars in the mouth of the cave, and . . . what then?
Would they take up a stone and . . .

Unthinkable, these new thoughts.

The two did think a good deal about the Others over
there, in their valley. They were the fathers of the New
One, and of the unborn infants, and of the little Monster
Astre had taken to the valley. Fathers . . . a word that
no one had needed, but now reverberated against the
sound of mothers. If these Clefts were not mothers,
then what were they? They were the mothers of Clefts
and Monsters, mothers of us all, our ancient mothers.

Take a half-grown Squirt and half-grown Cleft, and
if their middle parts were covered, no one could tell
the difference, but one would become a mother and
one a father. What a mother was they knew: Clefts had
a capacity the Others lacked; they could make new
people. What, then, was a father? They could tell any
young Cleft who would listen, or even the Old Ones,
that these new kinds of people made new infants, but
they could not say what it was the fathers added to
the mix. Which was there, in their arms, close to their
bodies, in Maire's infant, the New One.

We might think that the two were planning to take
that New One, and go off across the mountains to
the valley – not more than a walk, after all, but they
did not. The mysterious prompter was silent. Across
the mountain were brothers, if the Clefts down there
were sisters; and were fathers. There were no Old
Ones among the Squirts, no Old Hes. Well, that was

easy enough, there had not been enough time to make Old Ones in the valley. Young – old; that was easy enough. *Me* – the Clefts; *they* – the people once called Monsters.

The coming of these new people made comparisons start up in their minds, each idea with a shadow.

As for the Others, in their valley, they longed for the girls, whom they expected to come walking down the mountain any day. There were lookouts posted so that when they came they would be welcomed. And there were the eagles, too, who noticed everything. Sometimes the boys crept along the rocky hills so they could see the shore. They wanted to see Maire and Astre, but they did not recognise other individual Clefts.

The males – with their restless, ever-responding squirts, which were sometimes large, sometimes limp, but mostly stiff with need, so that it was unpleasant for them to bump into a bush or tall grass – did not know that their hungry wanting, their need, was the voice of their own Squirts down there, but felt as if it were their whole selves that wanted and needed. They fought each other, for no good reason, and invented games where they competed, sometimes dangerously. One of them, finding his squirt getting in the way, tied his loins up with eagles' feathers, and with leaves, and they began competing with each other to make the most attractive aprons. Soon they all wore decorative coverings and were ingenious in thinking up new ones.

Then something unexpected: two of the very oldest of them died. That is, two of the first Monsters, badly mutilated by the Clefts. They had watched arrive with the eagles, and then with the girls, babes just like themselves, but untorn, unhurt. They made their comparisons. They learned they were incomplete, misshapen, and so did the others. Their deaths took away a source of bitterness – of danger – which, only when it was gone, did they all recognise was better gone. And something else went with them – the baby language they had brought and taught to the very first boys. There were two ways of talking, one child-like, and the language learned from the visiting girls. With the two gone there was not so much left now of the infant talk. They all practised among themselves the language spoken by Maire and Astre. They were proud to be leaving behind infantile babble. But two had gone, disappeared, and there seemed to be far fewer of them, as if more than two had been removed. Perhaps they were the last of their kind? This was a thought the Clefts could never have: they had that gift, they gave birth to new Clefts and to Monsters too, but the boys, the males, could not make people.

They felt threatened. Yes, the eagles had brought them the two new baby Monsters, and they were thriving in the care of the doe, but . . . what were they going to do if more of them died? They were so vulnerable. Animals sometimes came raiding out of the forest, and more than once had taken off a boy. Boys at various times had been swept away by the river. They were too few: that was their situation. If two could die, for no reason – they had yet to take in the idea of old age – then why should not all of them just die? The records we have of that time speak of their fear.

They set watchers at night to see any animals coming out of the trees, and made piles of weapons where they could be easily reached. These were stones – they all could use stones to bring down even birds, or small animals. They could throw clubs and sticks; several of them together could outrun a small beast. But they knew some beasts working together could rush into their valley and take them all away – and there was nothing they could do.

When the girls did come running down the mountain they were welcomed with a hundred embraces but also with warnings: they must keep a watch for predators.

This visit went well, the boys were delighted, and the girls too, before they suddenly and as far as the boys were concerned inexplicably, took themselves off back to their shore. There they settled in caves near Maire and Astre, and this made a territorial statement of the fact that there were two parties now among the Clefts.

In the valley, with the Clefts gone, there seemed even fewer of them and almost at once two were lost: they went out into the trees after a much-liked fruit, and were attacked by a big animal they had not seen before. They ran, but not fast enough, and did not return to the valley.

The boys huddled near the great log, fearfully watching the margins of their valley. They even wondered if they could run over the mountain to the shore and persuade some more Clefts to come back with them.

Then the eagles came with the two newborn Squirts, two hungry babes. There had not been additions to their numbers for a time; and here were two, replacements for the two that had vanished into the forest. How to feed these hungry babes? The old doe had not been seen around recently. The eagles that had brought the babies stood in their places, watching the infants who lay crying noisily on the grass, stuffing their little fists into their mouths. The Clefts all had milk in those breasts of theirs, but they themselves had none. Then the old doe appeared from the forest's edge and stood looking at the two yelling babies. The boys cried out with joy but then with dismay: they could see that the animal's dugs were shrivelled and dry: she had no milk. She was really old: her muzzle and her ears were greying. She lifted her head and looked for a long time at the boys, and then at the eagles. Then she walked a little into the trees and called. A long silence, while still the hungry babies wailed. She called again and turned to greet two young does, nose to nose. It seemed she was telling them what to do, the three animals close, and then two fawns that had been afraid to come stood by the three big deer. The young does went to the babies and stood near, and looked at the big old doe – very probably their mother – then at the babes, then they looked long at the watching boys. The fawns began suckling. When the first doe, this old one, had come to rescue the first babies, she had lost her fawn. That must have been it: she lay down beside the babes to feed them. But fawns do not lie down to feed, they stand under the mother.

A boy crept close to a young doe, so that the fawn had to jump back away from him. He picked up a yelling babe and held it to a dug that dripped milk. The child did manage to take hold, and did suckle, a little, but the doe did not like what was happening, and her fawn didn't either. Before the other young doe could move away, the same boy held the second hungry baby to a teat. In this way both babes got a few mouthfuls of milk, but though the old doe did come right down close to the young does, and did nose first one babe and then the other, it seemed the animals simply decided to give up. They moved off, but before they left the boy snatched up a gourd and caught some leaking milk, and another boy did the same. There was a little supply of milk in the two gourds.

The old doe moved off slowly into the trees. She was lame, they could now see, and her head was not held up, but drooped, and the white scut of her tail did not friskily flick like those of the two young ones, but was limp and hung down.

These two boys had had no mothering at all, but had been nuzzled and licked and fed by this old doe now limping away from them. There was a lament from them which for a moment was louder than the babies' crying.

What were they going to do? The eagles recognised the difficulty and actually tore off little bits of fish which they tried to insert into the babies' mouths that were stretched wide with crying.

But over the mountain was the shore where lived the Clefts with their full milky breasts. Up the mountain the boys ran, down the other side, past the Killing Rock and burst out on to the rocks in full view of the basking Clefts. From the cave mouth just above, the two isolated ones saw them and called. Just as the Old Shes were ready to sit up and perhaps even attack, the two boys reached the cave where Maire and Astre were. They recognised Astre whom they had seen pregnant, but did not at once recognise Maire. The urgency of their mission made them incautious, and they bent to take up handfuls of these breasts, the life-saving breasts, and yes, there was milk. Maire and Astre understood why the boys had come: they had been wondering how the two babes had got on with feeding from the doe.

'What are you doing?' demanded Maire, and then Astre; and the boys answered, 'Milk, we need milk.'

Among the younger Clefts there had been a change. Of course the ones recently come back from the valley were not likely to respond but most of the others had crept up to the cave mouth and asked Maire and Astre about the other camp over there. And they had talked to the girls who had just come back. Whatever ferment that had gone to work in Maire and Astre was stirring in these young Clefts. We could call it curiosity, but perhaps there was more. However that was, while the two messengers from the valley stood there, staring down, fearful, ready to run, first one girl, then another, rose up from her patch of warm rock, and climbed up to the cave where Maire and Astre, watching as always, the First One, told the girls the situation. Two of the girls had full breasts. Perhaps they were even mothers of the two babes who were at that moment yelling their heads off in the valley.

'Go with them,' said Maire and Astre, and in a

moment the cave that had seemed full of people had again three, Maire and Astre and the First One. The two young women and the messengers found themselves urged on through the rocks. They were trying to run, these people who had never run in their lives.

They were fearful, of course they were; they were going over the mountain which had always been a barrier at the end of their world. And they did reach the mountain and did climb it and stood high among the eagles' nests, looking down into a wide valley where an energetic river bounded along. And down the mountainside they went, helped by the boys, and they were in the midst of the Monsters, now grown, or at least the same size as themselves, and the naked babes were being thrust at them, Monsters both, so they had to suppress repulsion and even fear.

The babes fastened on to those breasts as they had earlier tried to hold the does' dugs, and they fed, while all around stood the young Squirts, watching – not one had seen a baby feeding at a breast. Then, the babes sated, the boys took them, and placed them inside a shelter to sleep. And only then were the girls offered some water from the river, and some fruit and eggs that had been cooked on a hollow stone in the sun.

And then began the games that Maire and Astre had told them about, the Squirt and Cleft games, beginning with urgency and haste and then, as the boys, like the babes before them, were sated, continuing with the games of curiosity.

'What have you got there?', 'What is it', 'What is it for?', 'And you – what is that? Can I put my finger in?' And so on they went, as the Clefts lost their fear of the Monsters and began to be fascinated.

As for the two new Monsters or Squirts, they thrived and grew and were noisy, just like the First One in the cave with Maire and Astre.

These girls returned when their time was up to their shore and soon after that both Maire and Astre gave birth, a Cleft for one and a boy – the word had not yet been used – for the other.

The Old Ones were fearful, angry – and vindictive. They said that every female due to give birth must have a guard or a watcher who must kill every little Monster as it appeared.

And they did succeed in killing one. At once the eagles appeared, sweeping low over the heads of the frightened Clefts. Then the Old Ones demanded that the eagles be killed. This was absurd. How were the eagles to be killed? When a Cleft took up a beach stone and flung it at a seated eagle the pebble slid down over a glossy slope of feathers. The eagle, with its claws, tossed her into the waves. She swam: everyone knew how to swim. But then the big bird sat on the rocks just where the Cleft wanted to climb out, and pushed her back, and when she moved to a different point of exit, the bird moved too. She was ready to drown with exhaustion when the eagle at last flew up into the air letting her land. Everyone watched this little battle, fearful of what it meant. Everything seemed new and terrible. Fighting . . . animosity . . . retribution. The old females sat themselves up to see better, their mouths open in dismay, their little fat-swollen eyes full of hate.

There was no question, and they had to know it, of trying to kill an eagle. The birds were determined to prevent another murder of a child. And there were other new defenders: the girls who had recently returned from the valley were allied in their minds with the Squirts, and when labour and birth seemed imminent, positioned themselves ready to snatch up a babe as it appeared, to hand it to the waiting eagles.

There were always fewer of the old kind of Cleft. How many? But they did not say – or it wasn't recorded – 'We were Sixty and now we are Forty,' or even, 'We were many and now we are so few.' They did not say, 'Once all the caves were full and now half are occupied.' *Half* is a concept we take for granted. Why should they?

Over in the males' encampment they tended the new babes, and waited for more to arrive in the eagles' claws.

Maire and Astre during their pregnancies talked of

the males and their gift of life, which was so different from the Clefts'. They thought of the valley – with, yes, I think we can call it affection, though they never used the word or any similar one. No sooner were they over the births than they were ready to go off. For a long time they had not thought of going, but then they had to. They *had to*. Among all these mysteries, that surely is as important as any.

But it was not as easy now to leave. Astre's babe would have to be taken too, if they didn't want to entrust it to an eagle. They could not leave behind Maire's infant as once she would have done. They certainly could not leave on the shore the toddling child, the New One; unlikely, they knew, that she would be alive when they got back. Maire's new babe, Astre's boy, and the New One must all go. The two girls invited some of the younger Clefts who had shown an interest in the valley to come too. Four young women, one holding the New One, walked past the Killing Rock – where no one had been put out to die for a long time now – then on they went up the mountain. When they reached the top there were whoops and yells from the valley floor, and the boys came running up to greet the girls – who had to defend themselves, as otherwise they would have been raped (a word and a concept that would not appear for a considerable time). Fending off the hungry boys, they reached the valley floor and the

big social log. There something happened which illus-
trated so aptly the new sense that here were new
beginnings that it was told in the chronicles of both
parties. And reaches us in the crabby faded documents we call histories.

Maire's first mating had been with a Squirt whose
face she did not particularly notice, and nor did she
now, as he approached, knowing her. But the child
from that mating was here, and in her arms and as
usual making it impossible for anyone to ignore her.
And her face, this very young child's, was the same
as the young male's. Impossible not to notice: everyone
did. At first there was silence, which fell suddenly, as
they all came near to match the two faces, one a little
girl's or Cleft's, one the youth's. The owner of the
grown face, Maire's first mate, did not immediately
understand. Mirrors had not been invented or even
thought of. People knew how others looked, but not
much had been made of a large nose, or eyes too
close. But each of them must have seen their faces in
the slack lazy by-waters of the river, or even in a big
shell standing ready with water for the thirsty. Slowly
this young male, once a Monster now a handsome
youth, stood fingering his own face, then touching
the face of the child, who was pleased with the attention it was getting. Then the father, beginning to realise
what these matched faces meant, snatched the child
from Maire and ran off to the river bank. All followed,

watching as the youth knelt by the river where it made a pool, and looked down at himself and then at the child, mirrored there too. Then he handed the child back to Maire and walked, as it were blindly, certainly unsteadily, to the great log where he sat down. Maire sat by him, with the First One, and he kept looking at her, then at the child, then putting up his hands to touch his face. He was in a fever of wonderment – as they all were.

These three were a family, as we would know one, but what they made of it we may only guess. When the evening meal was finished and dark was falling over the valley, Maire and this youth and the child went to a shelter by themselves. That there was some sort of communion between them was evident, but what was it? What did it mean?

The girls who had come to help Astre and Maire entertained the youths, and they all talked of this great mystery, that mating could imprint a grown face on that of a child.

This visit to the valley, told and then much later written, was not likely to be forgotten, and plenty was said, speculation we would call it: the new people, the old former Monsters, had powers the old Clefts did not. Yes, a baby Cleft might resemble its mother – there were mothers and daughters in the first community – but now the people on the shore looked carefully at every face.

At that early stage none of the Clefts elected to stay in the valley. There was a suggestion that the valley was very warm, that the shelters were small and uncomfortable. The caves were large and airy, and sea breezes kept them fresh.

The girls went off to the valley when they had to, and returned knowing that they would in turn give birth. The boys waited for them. The Monsters were taken to the boys by the eagles, and now the deer did not feed them, the boys fetched Clefts. And all this went on, we do not know for how long. The laments of the boys that their numbers were falling ceased: for whatever reason, baby boys were born.

So, how long? Who knows, now?

And now this chronicler has a difficulty and it is to do with time, again: but much longer time than the complaint just above.

We Romans have measured, charted, taken possession of time, so that it would be impossible for us to say, 'And then it came to pass' . . . for we would have the year, the month, the day off pat, we are a defining people, but then all we know of events is what was said of them by the appointed Memories, the repeaters, who spoke to those who spoke again, again, what had been agreed long ago should be remembered.

This historian has no means of knowing how long the Clefts' story took to evolve. Astre and Maire, when first mentioned, were young Clefts, like the others, and then they thought of themselves as females, when the occurrence of the males made them have to compare and match, but for most of the records they were best known as figures from the ancient past. Their prominence in the tales, both male and female, the fact that it was Maire who gave birth to the First One, meant that their words were heard and then recorded. But soon they were not young females, but founders of families, clans, tribes – and at some point, ages later, evolved into goddesses. We know them under various names, but one is always associated with the star that is the patron of love and female witchery, and the other is an aspect of the moon. Their statues are in every town, village, glade, crossroads. Smiling, beneficent, queens in their own right, Artemis and Diana and Venus, and the rest, they are the most powerful intercessors between us and the heavens; we love them, we know they love us. But travellers may say that only a short horseback ride away, or a few days' walking, there are goddesses who are cruel and vengeful.

How long did it take for Astre and Maire to become more than themselves? We have no idea.

But one thing is certain: that once, very long ago, there was a real young woman who might have been called Maire, and then others, who were the first mothers of our race, carrying in their wombs the babes who were both Cleft and Other, both stuff of the very early people who, it is now thought, came out of the sea – and the new people, who brought restlessness and curiosity with them.

The girls who went to the valley and returned pregnant sat in the mouths of the caves and guarded their children, who were so different from the others. They walked early, talked early, and had to be watched every minute. Their mothers looked down at the rest of the tribe on the rocks, knew that their children had a double heritage, and noted the infants of the old kind were passive, easy, seldom cried, staying where they were set down; they were active only when they were put into the water, where they swam about and were fearless.

When the new mothers wanted to swim, they went all together, carrying their infants, and chose pools not used by the rest of the Clefts, who had split into two parts, one always watching what the other was doing.

Something else happened, which is hardly mentioned in the old chronicles. It was taken for granted, and that means fire must have been there for a long time.

In the valley a fire burned always, not far from the log, and it was kept alive, with special attendants. Soon fires were burning outside the caves. These fires appearing are one reason to question the possible timescales that have been suggested.

No fires at all – neither on the shore nor in the valley – and then, always, fires. When fire first appeared that must have been as much of a shock as the new babies that seem to have come from nowhere.

Why, suddenly, fire? Certainly for many generations they had seen lightning strike a spark off the edge of a rock into dry leaves, or lightning had flashed into a patch of dry grass and an old log had caught fire and burned there, perhaps for days. Someone walking in the trees had stumbled into an area black on cracked earth, with the charred remains of little animals. Someone might have seen a locust cooked in flames, eaten it, thought: that's nice. Had they tried a roasted mouse or a bird's egg cooked in a hollow of a rock as the flames went over it? But not once had this person, or any of them, thought: I'll take a part of that burning log to where we live and it will warm us at night, it will cook our food.

Then, suddenly, precisely that thought entered an early mind, or all of them, took possession – and then a great fire burned in the valley bottom, and outside the cave mouths fires burned in the shelter of a great rock as the early people crouched near it. For a long time no fires, then fires, and nuts were roasted and eggs, and perhaps the birds who made the eggs.

Not these people, not the first males – the Squirts – but that name would go, just as had the Monsters.

A memory remained of how it was a doe who fed and warmed the first monstrous babes. There were people of the eagle, people of the deer, so whatever meat was charred on the early fires it was never eagle or deer.

We may easily look back now and see those early youths around the great fire and brood about that mystery – which we do not know how to answer – which was that for ages – long ages, as long as you like – those early people saw fire frisking about in bushes, leaping in the trees, flashing down from clouds, something familiar to them, like river water, but never thought they could tame it, but then suddenly they did. Perhaps 'suddenly' is not right, perhaps it should be 'slowly'. What causes these changes where something impossible then becomes not only allowed, but necessary? I tell you, to think about this phenomenon for long leads to a disquiet that drives away sleep and makes you doubt yourself. In my lifetime things that were impossible have become what everyone accepts – and why. But *why*? Did these old people ever think, 'We have known fire as part of the life of the forest, but now it does our bidding – how did that happen?' There is no record of it.

Meanwhile in the valley the young males are still nervous about their numbers. Fire, that great benefice, has not added to their safety. The hazards in great forests go on: a charging boar, or an angry bear; a snake that doesn't have time to get out of the way of those naked feet; a boulder rolls down a hillside; someone unused to fire sets a handful of burning grass in an unburned place and does not run fast enough to avoid the bounding, leaping flames; poison from plants and insect bites. And the river flowing there is deep and easily sweeps away an incautious child.

There is a record that fire brought anger and scolding from Maire and from Astre. A toddler staggered into the flames: he was not stopped in time. Maire, arriving for her visit with them, told them they were inconsistent. They complained about how few they were, how seldom the eagles brought them babies, but they did not watch their little children.

This was not the first time they were scolded.

Earlier, a young doe stepped down to the river's edge to drink, and behind her crawled one of the babes she was feeding. As the doe drank, dipping her muzzle into the water, the child, emulating her, doing as his mother was doing – she was that – leaned too far over the edge and fell in.

'Why don't you set people to watch your infants, why don't you keep guard?'

The histories of the females record their incredulity: they simply could not understand the carelessness of the boys who did dangerous and foolish things.

There are remarks in the females' records that the boys were clumsy, seemed to lack a feeling for their surroundings, and were inept and did not understand that if they did *this*, then *that* would follow.

But all this time – and who knows how long that was? – a threat continued worse than the dangers of the forest, the river, the fires – it was the animosity of the Old Females and a section of the Clefts who supported them. We have the record of an event that has the texture of improbability, so that it is hard to make it mesh with the rest.

An Old Female climbed to the top of the mountain 'to see for herself'. We have the exact words, and how much do they reveal? What a suspicious mind was there, hearing all kinds of descriptions from the young ones, of the events going on in the valley where the Monsters grew and flourished. She had not believed what she was told, that is clear. Hard for us to put ourselves into that cautious old mind. She was one of a species which for long ages had lived on the edge of that warm sea, never moving from it, and the horizon of her mind was limited by the mountain that bounded their world. Yes, she had always looked into a scene of ocean, of waves, the movement and tumble of them, but how can we imagine a mind whose thoughts were limited to a strip of rocky shore? For all her life this creature had not done more than sag from her sleeping cave to the rocks where she lay sunning herself, and from there to loll in the sea, and from there back again; she had scarcely moved in her life and yet now she decided to go to the mountain 'to see for herself'. Had a drop of that new fever that had forever altered some of the young females danced for a moment in her veins? Or was it that she had no concept of the difficulty of her moving, she who never moved?

The scenes she and her forebears had known for always had changed. Outside the caves where Maire and Astre and others of the new kind lived with their infants the great fires burned. She and her kind had seen fire flick over the crests of waves, strike across skies, burn in chains along the tops of the little hills behind the shore, but fire as a familiar – never. Now the fires at night were sometimes so tall that fish and sea animals rose to the sea's surface goggling, because the light of the flames was gilding the waters, and they wondered if the moon or the sun had risen out of turn. The light of the fires running in the hollow of the waves told the Old Ones that nothing they knew was the same, and that the new held dangers for them they had learned already.

Yet, she would see for herself. She heaved herself up on to her great flabby feet, and supported by the young females who remained loyal to the old ways, staggered off the rocky beaches, and then slowly, step after step, directed herself to the mountain. Before she had moved a few steps she was grumbling and groaning. Before she had even reached the Killing Rock she had to sit and rest. But up she did get, and on she went, across the uneven and stony ground, away from the sea, her element, her safety, and with most of her weight on her supporters she did go on, always more slowly, always stopping. The young ones were begging her to turn back, but she persisted and that in itself had to make us wonder. Perhaps it was only because she had no conception of walking such a distance that she could make herself go on.

At the foot of the mountain she did let herself down out of those supporting arms, and sit, moaning, but then she dragged herself up. Often on her hands and knees, she crawled up the mountainside. By now the eagles screamed around her, and flapped down close to her and away. She screamed at them, they screamed at her, these enemies who had wanted to kill each other. What could she be thinking of these birds, taller than she was, birds who could lift a young Cleft off the rocks and drop her into the waves? The noise of her ascent was quite frightful, what with her groans and cries and imprecations and shrieks of hate at the birds, the stones she dislodged that bounded off the mountain, the encouraging cries of the young ones. At the top she was among the eagles' nests, and all around her on the rocks, in the sky above her, were the great birds. She stood, held up by the young Clefts, and looked into the valley, but what could she see with eyes used to focusing on the rough and tumble of waves? But she did try to look and to understand.

There were shelters down there, but she had never seen anything of the kind. They were made of boughs and screens of river grass, and she could see a dark movement, capped with little white crests, but she did not know it was a river. She had been told there was a big river in the valley, but for her waves tossed and when the wind was rough, rampaged, but it was not easy to think of water confined between banks moving fast from the mountain down to barriers of rock that in fact concealed the waves from her. Down there were people, and there was an enormous fire. They were so few: she was used to seeing the rocks around her covered with basking Clefts. A lot, many, and she was seeing so few. She knew they were Monsters, because she had been told that was what she would see. Some of the boys and some visiting Clefts were in the river, swimming. Some new baby Monsters were with the others down there, but they were inside the shelters. That scene down there, in the valley she had imagined populated, was disappointing her, as we are when imagined armies of enemies, or even crowds, dissolve away in daylight.

She was here, after that awful journey up the mountain; she 'had seen for herself', but there was nothing to see. She did not like the look of that fast wave-topped river; nor the fire, which was fed by dead trees from the forest and was enormous, sending up a column of smoke almost to the height where she stood. She could not make herself go down into the valley, now that she was here. Everything she saw seemed hostile to her. She was aching, ill with the effort she had made. She stood, fanning herself with a frond of dead leaves in her great arm and fatty hand, and she wailed. Her wailing disturbed the scene down there. She watched a few of the Monsters detach themselves from the fire scene and begin climbing towards her. She wailed again because she feared them, and because she could hardly move. She sank on to the earth and moaned; and when the young men came, they saw not only the Old Female, whom they knew they must fear, but young Clefts they did not know. They believed these had come as earlier ones had, with friendly intentions, and so they were grinning and reaching out their hands to these unknown females.

But the old woman screamed because she was so close to these Monsters, although they were wearing feathers and leaves from their waists, concealing what she feared. The young Clefts, screaming, ran off down the mountain towards their shore, and so the Old She was abandoned, with the angry eagles so close all around her on their tall rocks, and the boys, her enemies. Who now did something unexpected, seeing that she was the enemy. They conferred, standing there in a group, still gazing after the girls who were by now far away running towards their shore. Close by was an old tree, and it had shed some branches. The boys pulled a large dead branch to the old woman, dragged her on to it, then pulled her back down the mountainside, while she shrieked and complained. The eagles kept them company, floating immediately overhead. The Old Female was clinging on to the branch, bouncing up and down over rough places and stones. She cried and whimpered, and once did fall off and had to be lifted back on. It took all the boys' strength to get her down to the level of the Killing Rock. There they left her and went back up the mountain to their valley.

The girls currently visiting the boys asked why they had gone to the rescue of the Old She. They seemed surprised they were asked. 'But she was crying,' they explained at last.

Now it had to be remembered that the boys never let the babies cry. A noisy or weeping little Monster made the older ones quite frantic. All the Clefts had to remember how the first Monsters screamed when the Clefts tormented and teased them – and worse.

What were they remembering when one of the babes yelled?

'She was making such a noise . . .' said the boys. Then, 'She was upsetting the baby eagles.' 'Yes, the baby eagles were frightened.'

These explanations came first, then came what seemed to be the real reason. 'Those Clefts, they were just stupid, letting the Old One cry. It was so easy: we just put her on the branch and pulled her down and that was that. The Clefts never thought of it.'

The fact that the Old She reached the rock bruised and even bloodied did not concern the boys. What mattered was their achievement, and one that showed up the stupidity of the Clefts.

The episode became 'Silly Clefts. They didn't know what to do to rescue the Old One.'

About now began records of how the Clefts discussed the boys, always on the lines of 'But why did they do that? They do such funny things, the boys.'

We are talking about only some of the Clefts, the friends of Maire and Astre; others shuddered when they mentioned the inhabitants of the valley.

It was established that the boys were 'silly', were clumsy.

But we have not finished with the Old She who had wanted to see for herself. The bumps and bruises took time to heal, and she did not forgive the girls who ran away leaving her, as she saw it, to the mercy of her enemy. These girls taunted the others who went to the valley and mated with the Squirts and though, one after another, they changed and became like the others, 'Maire's girls', there was hostility and many incidents of spitefulness that were recorded in the annals.

The other Old Females were not mentioned: it was only the instigator of the trip up the mountain. We may make what we can of this. And it was this Old Female who made the plan which could have destroyed not only the Squirts, or most of them, but also a lot of the girls. Not immediately. First, that slow old brain had to deal with the fact that the girls ran away down the mountain because they feared to be raped. Although Maire had tried to explain what she believed the 'Monsters' were for, their possible function as progenitors, the Old Ones did not take that in. And it was hard for them. First, the advent of the Monsters had caused the new children, disliked and feared by all the old Clefts. And then the 'rapes' caused both baby Clefts and baby Monsters. The baby Clefts were Clefts, whether 'difficult' or not, and the Monsters were the same as those she had seen on the top of the mountain, people, and not Clefts, behind their skirts of feathers and leaves.

Very interesting it is, what people can take in and what they can't. In the Old Females it was because they couldn't. A new, quicker mind had been born into that community of shore-dwelling females, together with the tincture of maleness. The old, slow, suspicious mind understood one simple fact: everything that had happened to change the old ways, caused such division and malice between the different parts of the Clefts, was because of the Monsters. It was as simple as that: the Monsters were the enemy. And now they had to be got rid of.

The Old She sent one of her girls to tell Maire to come and see her. She sent nods and smiles to Maire who was sitting in the mouth of her cave. Maire merely nodded back. She was in no hurry to go. She did not want to seem obedient to the Old Females, whom she suspected of wishing (and plotting) harm.

Maire was with the New One and some children. A lot of people were watching to see if she was going at once to the Old She. Maire was consoling the babes, as always fretting noisily. Down on the rocks by the sea the girls who supported the Old Shes lay about, half in and half out of the water. They looked up at Maire and hated her. Maire was responsible for the divided tribe, the bad temper of the Old Shes, the new demanding babies. And from the rocks above the caves were some boys watching too. Maire could not make sense of their being there and her alarm, already strong, was strengthened. She was afraid for them, just as she was these days for the safety of the new children.

It could not be said that maternal feelings were strong in those early females. It was recent, that children were precious, full of promise or threat.

She thought a good deal about the children and, too, about the boys in the valley. What she felt was, in fact, pity, a tender protectiveness, though these ideas – and the words – were not available to her. Those poor Monsters, the poor boys, she was so sorry for them. What she felt for them was the equivalent of putting her arms round them and holding them safe – as she did with the New One. She and her band of girls lived in these tall, airy caves, with their clean sandy floors, and outside the great fires they had learned from the boys to build and keep burning, they who were so skilled at making and tending their fires. Those poor Monsters lived in their sheds and shelters, which were always full of rubbish and smelled bad, because they simply did not have the knack of keeping order. There they were on the very edge of the great forest from where at any moment (and this had happened much more than once) a beast could leap out and grab a babe or even a half-grown boy. She thought of the poor Squirts, and meanwhile kept an eye on the boys clustering on the tops of the hills above the shore. She was thinking:

keep out of sight, fools – don't you know you are in danger?

Now Maire, at her leisure, rose, telling the children she would soon be back, and walked down to the Old Females.

And now, dear Roman reader, what do you see in your mind's eye, watching Maire on her descent? But I'll tell you, you will be seeing what is in my mind now, our minds, full with images of our goddesses. My father's best slave, bought for a high price because of his skills, knew how to make copies of loved statues. In the olive grove near our house was a statue of Diana, my father's favourite. There she was, in her little frisking skirt, holding the bow of gilded wood my father used to joke would not be able to bring down a sparrow. And at the junction of our road with the main road stood Artemis, not made by our slave, but he copied it, smaller, and the copy was in the olive grove too. I see a tall, graceful female, with her elegant little head, her knot of gleaming hair, bound by a silver fillet whose ends flutter in the sea breeze, released from the rigidity of metal by our imaginations. Her robe, of gentlest linen, floats about her. Her sandalled feet step lightly among the stones of the shore. She is smiling. We all know the goddess smile, promising our protection now and for ever. It is not possible to imagine anything that could banish Artemis, or for that matter pretty Diana, from their positions in our hearts. For ever will our smiling goddesses stand on guard against all the perils that confront us.

But those who watched Maire walking down from her cave mouth saw nothing like this. We do not know what the Clefts looked like. We do not know what this Cleft, this female, the first ever to give birth to a babe carrying the blood of both Clefts and Squirts, the first of a new race, ours, humans, was like in build, height, bearing.

We can make a safe guess Maire was no slim girl, no Diana. These first people on the shore: they probably were sea creatures once. But all of them, the Clefts, were in sea water as much as they were out of it. It was not unknown for them to sleep rocking on gentle waves, arms afloat, their faces turned up to the sky. They swam – well, like fishes or sea beasts. It is safe to say they were stocky in build, with heavy shoulders and arms, big thighs and muscular working buttocks. Sea creatures carry a useful layer of fat. Maire would have had strong white teeth: they ate raw fish, biting the flesh off the bones. To come on a group of Clefts squatting over a catch of fish, biting and gnawing, it would have been easy at first glance to think them seals or porpoises. This female, Maire, our first mother ancestor, whose name was for the moon, had large soft breasts full of milk: we know this from the very first oral records we have from the Squirts, the males, who loved the Clefts' big milky breasts.

This squat, solid, healthy female reached the Old Shes lying out on their rocks like stranded fish, and she smiled and said, 'There are things we need to talk about' – taking the initiative away from them. Maire knew she was in danger: the smell and tension of threat was strong. She knew there was a plot of some kind. If she, Maire, wanted to get rid of, let's say, Astre and girls loyal to them, then what would she do? It would be necessary to trick them into some deep pool, and then get the Old Females' girls to drown them, pulling them under. Not easy, no; since everyone swam so well. But it would be necessary to take the victims by surprise.

Maire half expected what she would hear next. The Old Ones wanted Maire and Astre to take both 'their' girls, and the ones allied to them, the Old Ones, away for a trip.

And now Maire heard the bones of the plot. They would make an expedition along the shore to a certain beach to gather clams, and then to another beach, to get supplies of a certain seaweed. So, she was right: Maire's nerves had already told her. At some point she, Astre and the girls who were their friends would be enticed into the sea and killed.

Meanwhile, all this time, on the rocky hills, the

visiting boys still hung about, watching. 'Why were they there?' 'How had they been got there?' A couple of the great eagles floated above the boys, watching: they knew there was danger, and Maire waved at the boys, ignoring the Old Females, meaning, 'Go; leave. Why do you think the eagles are up there?' The boys waved back: they had not understood.

Maire told the old women that the trip would provide the giant clams and seaweed, and went back up to her cave, full of worry: she simply could not understand what the boys were doing up there.

Astre and a friend were making up their fire for the night.

The boys were there, so dangerously close – because it was some time since girls had gone to the valley. No Monsters had been born recently. What does that 'recently' mean? We don't know. How much I do admire us Romans' careful way with measurement and time, when wrestling to understand old chronicles of people who never thought: A month ago, In a week's time . . . Once . . . When . . .

Perhaps the Old Shes thought that maybe there would not be any more Monsters born. An appropriate kind of thought for their slow old minds: 'If no Monsters born *recently* then perhaps there won't be any more.'

Very well: some things were clear. The Old Ones

wanted Maire and Astre to go right away, with their allies, the new kind of babes and children, and the Old Females' girls would go too. They planned to get rid of the new people who had new thoughts and who gave birth to the new children. Then the rule of the Old Shes would be unchallenged and there would be no more girls like Maire and Astre, and no 'new ones'.

Why were the boys up there on the rocks of the hills?

They did not like being too close to the Clefts' shore, and were afraid of the Old Females.

This seemed to Maire like a warning in itself; if she knew why the boys were there she would understand what the threats were. Of course, she could ask one of 'her' girls to ask one of the Old Females' girls what was afoot. That is, what was planned for the boys: she knew or was pretty sure what was intended for them, the girls.

The truth was that an Old She – the adventurous one – had ordered her girls to entice the boys down to the cliffs above the shore, but her plan – to destroy the boys – had so far misfired.

An excursion to the big-clam beach would take several days, plenty of time for occasions to drown Maire and Astre and their babes, and their allied girls. It was the simplicity of this plan that had to be admired. But the rest of the Old Ones' intentions were dark indeed. It was not possible for the Old Ones' girls to harm the boys, who were much faster runners and could defend themselves with sticks and stones. Bows and arrows too, these days. A direct fight could only end in victory for the boys, particularly as the boys' allies, the eagles who watched over them, would fight on their side.

Maire, Astre and their followers talked it all over and came to no conclusion. If they did get one of the Old Shes' girls to come and talk to them, the Old Females would know their plans were suspected. It would be easy to entice a girl up to Maire's cave. There was no absolute division between the obedient girls and the rebels. After all, Maire's and Astre's allies had once been followers of the Old Shes. Many of the obedient ones had come to Maire's cave to ask what was so attractive about the Monsters. Some had gone to the valley to find out for themselves. So long did the clam gatherers' party delay their departure that the Old Shes sent a message to ask what was keeping them.

We do not know how many Clefts set off together, only that their children went with them. As they walked along the edge of the sea they knew they were being spied on: one of the Old Shes' girls kept pace with them, hiding in the rocks. That meant it was not possible to do what they had planned, which was to walk until nightfall, when they could creep back towards their shore in the dark, and find some high place where they could watch what was happening. The Old Shes' girls would report back to them.

Next day the party dawdled and delayed, keeping the children with them, and then they saw that nearly all the hostile girls had disappeared in the night. From this Maire and Astre realised that the plan to dispose of them and their children was not the primary one.

Maire, Astre and some others waited until dark, then made their way to a low hill from where they could see their own shore and, on the near side, the Killing Rock, and the great cliff where there was the pit where once girls had been thrown as sacrifices.

This place, once honoured for its associations with killing and presumably a deity of some kind, made Maire think hard about what she knew about it. Not much. The tall hill or peak, perhaps volcanic in origin, had on its seaward side The Cleft, where the red flowers flowed, in its season. The Cleft was the deity, we believe now, matching and echoing the red flow of the Clefts, associated as it was with the moon. When we look back into the origin of our gods, it is not always easy to say specifically what was divine. We do not expect to climb up the slopes of Mount Olympus! Or to see Venus step up out of the waves!

But this Cleft had about it an air of dread, of fear, although its top was not even hard to reach. On the seaward side was The Cleft and the cave from where it was possible to look through cracks and crevices to see the skeletons, the skulls, the white dust of the bones. But on the other side a path wound gently up. At the very top was a flattish rim, but inside this rim was a platform, where so many girls had stood trembling before they had been flung down into the ossuary. More than the odours of decay rose up from the depths. There were vapours that at first confused and then anaesthetised the girls, who were unconscious when they were pushed down. The reason why we, the males, believed this practice had ceased was precisely because Maire and Astre and their allies did not think of this place when they puzzled over what the Old Ones were planning. It is probable that it was so long since sacrifices had happened there that everyone had forgotten it.

When the light came they could see a wide sweep from the plains of the sea to the mountain that led to the boys' valley. Nothing was moving. Far away on their shore tiny spots and dots showed that not all the girls had set off on the clam gathering. A couple of eagles swung in their circles over the mountain. And then, but not until midday, a group of the enemy girls came from their rocks, slowly enough, taking their time, and paused on the Killing Rock, as if unwilling to go on. How many? The word used was 'several'. Slowly they left the Rock, and slowly went to the foot of the mountain. There they began to climb. None of these girls had been before to the valley, though some had accompanied the Old She who had wanted to see for herself. They had been too occupied supporting the Old One, calming her, to notice much of the way. They were very slow in their progress up the mountain, possibly because the eagles were screaming at them. When they reached the top they stood there, looking down at the valley with its frightening river. Why were they lingering there? From the valley came whoops and shouts, and in a moment the boys were up there too. The girls were shaking their breasts and performing enticing movements with their hips, which were probably being used for the very first time. Now at last it was clear that the Old Ones, or one of them, had understood what Maire had told them. The girls had been told to attract the Squirts, to lure them. But for what end?

When the boys appeared on the mountain top the girls had already begun their descent away from them. Then, taking a good look, they stopped in surprise. The boys wore their narrow aprons of feathers and leaves. If some of the girls had visited the valley before they would have seen the boys naked, perhaps just come from the river – seen them in their Monster guise. Now what they feared, or perhaps desired, was hidden. The truth was, these girls hardly recognised the Squirts, these smiling young males, decorated, and their hair combed long and sleek. Maire had given the boys combs, made from the skeletons of fish, and told them how to care for their hair. The girls were looking at handsome young men, but did not know that what they felt was admiration. So, instead of running away so the boys could follow, they stood, stunned by surprise. At last they did run off down the hill, and the boys ran after them, calling and shouting as if chasing an animal to kill it. They ran much faster than the slow girls. That they did not at once catch the girls was because they were making a game of the chase.

What the watchers from their hill saw was girls, mostly the Old Ones' allies, running as fast as they could, the boys after them.

Maire and Astre and their allies took time to understand. The girls had been instructed to entice the boys – but why?

By the time the two, pursued and pursuers, had reached the Killing Rock, the boys were just behind the girls, who stopped, stood and faced the boys. After what they had heard from the girls who visited the valley, they would know that rape would ensue, but if you have never experienced penetration, consensual or not, what then do you expect? Rape is not an accomplished skill, like eating. The girls were now undecided: they had been given instructions to lure the boys, but now what?

Up on the hill, the watchers knew it was time for them to descend and intervene, even if they did not know why.

The girls and boys appeared to be exchanging amiable taunts. The boys were attempting to grab hold of the girls, particularly their breasts. For the first time, the Squirts were matched with an equal number of girls.

Then the girls freed themselves and, without running, or seeming to try to escape, they made for the path that went up the cliff at whose top was the opening of the pit. And now at last Maire and Astre and the others understood. Not all at once – and this is where we have to think that the sacrificial role of The Cleft was well in the past, a part of old history. The foul odours that the pit emitted, or the caves at the foot, were always mentioned in any story about it, but the deadly miasmas were not always mentioned. But as soon as it was put like this, the girls are luring the boys up to the pit's edge so they can be pushed in, since the boys were stronger by far than the girls the next thought had to be: Of course, they say there are the deadly vapours.

Now the watchers, Maire and Astre, were running as fast as they could. They could see the boys were being persuaded up the path to the top, while the girls came behind, smiling and friendly.

It was not a cliff so tall that it must take a long

time to get up it, and soon the young men would be at the top of the path. There at the edge of the great hole, or ancient volcano, was a broad ledge, flat and worn by who knows how many long ages of feet, of people, standing there to supervise the horrid rituals of sacrifice. The platform where the victims must stand to take in their paralysing dose of fatal gases was a short way down inside. The boys were delighting in the difficulties of the climb and the eminence up here, from where they could see ocean and mountain and the eagles, and they turned to admire and, seeing the girls just below, smiled and stretched out their arms. The girls saw them. They were beautiful, these very young men, these boys, these Monsters, the objects of their hate . . . but what had they been hating? Now the girls should have run away down the path to the foot of the climb, leaving the boys, having done their work of getting them up there. Then one girl, and then another, began to cry. They wept and stretched out their arms as if beseeching them to . . . well, save themselves. 'Save yourselves,' Maire and Astre were shouting. They knew the boys well enough to know that in a minute they would be jumping down from the lip of the pit to the platform, because it was there, because it was a challenge and difficult.

The girls were screaming at the boys, 'Come down, stop, stop, come back.'

All the girls were screaming and stretching out their arms, and crying.

One or two had yelled at them to jump down on the platform: not all the young females had seen the boys were beautiful . . . not a word they had ever associated with them. And there was excitement, now, in watching the boys leap. The girls were excited by the boys. They were experiencing desire, some of them.

Maire was climbing up the path, Astre just behind her, and others behind them. The whole cliff face was crowded with young females. The boys knew Maire and Astre, the oldest of their visiting females, the females with their breasts full of milk, teachers, instructors – friends – and when the two yelled at them to come back they wanted to do what they were told. But one boy, unable to resist danger, had leaped down on to the platform. As Maire and Astre reached the circling ledge where the boys crowded, their pioneer, perhaps the first person ever to jump inside the cone of a volcano just for the hell of it, swayed and fell. If he had fallen one way he would have toppled into the gulf where piled bones told their story. Maire jumped down to the platform, dragged him, together with Astre, back up to the lip where the fresh air revived him. Now it was necessary to explain to the young males what the enticing females had been after – their deaths.

Some of the youths had already slunk away down

and some of the girls had too, and were off to their shore.

Maire and Astre pulled at the boys, tugged them away from the pit's edge. It was a scene of great confusion for them all. The boys had been seeing smiling and friendly Clefts, but had not yet taken in they had been trying to kill them, and here were their old friends, Maire and Astre and other Clefts they knew well. The boys did descend the path, because of Maire's and Astre's urging but all around were Clefts who were not well known to them. Which were friends? Which were their enemies?

Reaching the Killing Rock, there was a general mêlée of friendly embraces, which then became what we call an orgy. But the very notion of an orgy implies the breaking down, the disruption, of an agreed order. How can you have an orgy – even use the word? – when there had never been even the suggestion of off limits, of partialities, of preferences, let alone customs and habits.

A couple of the girls who had lately been enticing the boys to their deaths, now saw what was going on and returned to join in.

An Old Female, supported by a couple of girls who had run back to their shore, came because of the noise, and saw what she thought was a scene of general violence and even murder. She began shouting encouragement at her girls to hurt the boys if they could. Her presence slowly impressed itself on the youths and then she saw faces turn towards her, the dawning of the realisation that here was the instigator of attempted murder. Her own girls knew this truth and soon told the other girls, and then the youths understood too.

She was alone. Maire and Astre were engaged with youths whom we could accurately call the fathers of their children, and they were not able to see what was going to happen. A Squirt – he who had lost consciousness for a while up there on the platform – picked up a stone and crashed it on her head. The first murder recorded in the annals of the males (the very first was forgotten) was on that day. Probably there were others, and we are not mentioning the killing of the very early, the first-born Monsters.

The carcass of the Old She was thrown on to the Killing Rock for the eagles.

The boys went back to their valley: some of the girls were with them. Maire and Astre returned to their caves. Or tried to.

In the meantime something else had happened. When Maire and Astre left their lookout point that morning, the children and infants were put in the charge of friendly Clefts, who could not have known much of what was going on. At various times they saw the Old Ones' girls tempting the boys down the mountain, and the boys making a game of it all. At one point it seemed the cliff of The Cleft was clustered with girls, but it was not easy to see if they were the Old Ones' allies, or Maire's and Astre's. They saw what looked like a battle going on all over the Killing Rock. They did not see the death of the Old She. Girls who could have been either the Old Ones' allies, or Maire's and Astre's, streamed back to their shore. Then a lot of the boys, with some girls, went past and up the mountain. Next, eagles came swooping down from the mountain to the Killing Rock.

The infants and children in their lookout were by now complaining and fretful. No messenger had come to say what was going on. In the end this group of girls with the children left their lookout and went down to the level of the Killing Rock, where a great number of eagles had assembled, tearing with their beaks and claws at pieces of meat that certainly were not infants. The eagles frightened the children, who soon were crying loudly. This noisy band made its way back to the shore, where their way was barred by enemy girls, who threw stones at them, and even at the children. The Old Females at the sea's edge were gesturing and threatening: it was clear they were ordering their girls to catch the children and dispose of them – the sea was very near. The girls minding the children could not run away: precisely because of the children, even when it was evident their own

132

harm was intended. They stood at the limit of the shore and called to the Old Ones to help them. 'Help us' – they did not know about the plot to do away with them on the clam-gathering trip, nor of the plan to kill off the boys. The Old Ones had not been friendly to Maire and Astre and their girls for a long time, but there was no reason to suspect plans for murder.

When these girls wanted to climb up to their caves with the children, their way was barred by the enemy Clefts – it was from this moment that there were two groups of Clefts, evident enemies, out to harm each other. The girls with the children fought their way through the hostile girls, their helplessness making them defiant and brave. They got themselves into Maire's and Astre's cave and stood at the entrance, with their sticks and stones. The stacked firewood now came in useful.

Maire and Astre arrived to find their girls and the children and infants in the cave, with a crowd of the enemy girls outside, taunting and threatening the defenders, while the Old Shes, from the sea's edge, shouted encouragement.

The two groups were evenly matched: this we have to deduce, since this battle went on until the dark came and they could hardly see each other. Maire left the cave, making sure the children were safe, and walked through the threatening girls down to the

sea's edge and the Old Females, who knew that one
of their number had apparently disappeared, but not
how and where. There Maire told them the Old Shes
could not expect to live for very long if there were
any more killings, or even talk about killings. In the
account of this scene, much is made of the arrival of
the eagles, fresh from the Killing Rock, who sat along
the tops of the cliff, looking down at the Old Shes.
Threateningly, says the tale. By now, so the story-
teller goes on, Maire and Astre were considered by
the eagles as friends to the boys and therefore their
friends too. The episode, both in our – males' –
records and in the Clefts', is called 'The Arrival of
the Eagles' – making it sound as if this cowed the
Old Shes and made them at least apparently amenable.

But Maire was thinking it would be a good thing
to get the hated new children well away from this
dangerous shore, at least for a time. Maire walked
back to the mouth of her cave, unarmed except for
the authority her nature, her being, gave her and,
ignoring the hostile girls who were insulting the babes
and children for their noise and 'the trouble they gave
everyone', she called to the besieged ones to come
out. Then this group, telling their friendly girls where
they were going, walked off past the Killing Rock,
still occupied by eagles, and up the mountain and
down to the valley where they were awaited.

The children would be safer here, provided they

were well watched to stop them falling into the river, or wandering off into the trees.

All these children had heard tales about the kindly does who fed the babes when there was no adult Cleft around and it was hard to keep them, those who were walking, away from the forest.

This event, or events, of the Old Shes' plot to entice the boys into the deadly airs of The Cleft, their intention to kill as many of Maire's allies as could be done, plans to harm the children, were recorded in detail that is vivid even now, but it is the last for some time of the definite, the particular, of *then* dissolved into its separate moments. That so long-ago day made such an impression, not only on the storytellers but in the memories of the participants, that we can see them still. Or could, if we knew what these people, our so remote ancestors, really looked like.

Now, reading the words that were first spoken by people who were not so far removed from the time, we came up against . . .

'And then . . .' 'But *when*?'

'Next . . .' 'After *what*?'

'Soon . . .' 'How long after . . . ?'

And now this historian, previous historians and all future chroniclers must find ourselves brought to a stop. The records, crabbed and cracked and faulty as they are, tell some kind of tale, with that internal logic, not always perceived at once, that seems a guarantee of verisimilitude. And then – the story stopped. Certain themes continued, for instance, the enmity of the Old Ones towards the new. The growing together in mind and cooperation of the two kinds of people, Clefts and their offspring – for the former Monsters in the valley were that. These were prosperous, easy-living, comfortable communities, and for a long time the eagles watched over them all. But then – the records ended. But we must remember what ended. If history depended on oral records, on Memory, on the Memories, then no easy process terminated. First of all, a community, a people, must decide what sort of a chronicle must be kept. We all know that in the telling and retelling of an event, or series of events, there will be as many accounts as there are tellers. An event should be recorded. Then it must be agreed by whoever's task it is that this version rather than that must be committed to memory. The tale must be rehearsed – and we may amuse ourselves imagining how these must have been, often, acrimonious, or at least in dispute. Whose version of events is going to be committed to memory by the Memories? So, at last, the tale, the history is finished, to the point where no one will actively dispute it. Then comes the process of listening, while the history is spoken aloud. In a cave somewhere? At least well away from the sounds of the sea or of a forest when a wind is blowing. The tale is told, is lodged in the minds of the Memories, probably several of them. And at specified intervals someone – or several – asks for the history to be told again to be checked by people who had lived through it all. Is the tale still there? It has not become blurred? Nothing has been forgotten? And then this checked and verified tale is told carefully to the next in the line to hold the tribes', the people's, history. This is quite a process, is it not, and one that involves everyone.

No, an oral history must, as soon as you think about it at all, be the creation and then the property of a people. Imagine, for instance, who – and how – agreed to record the contest between the Old Females and Maire, whoever she was that held that name in that time. We may be sure that Old Shes would not agree with Maire's version of events. Who made the decision that this and that Cleft, and not another or others, should hold the history in her mind? And the same is true for our people, the boys. Our records were full of anecdotes, sharply remembered events involving the Old Females, who certainly would not agree with one single word agreed on by us.

We have to account for the fact that both Clefts, and we, kept records, with all the attention and care it involved, for – and here I go – for ages. For a long time. And then what happened?

Some think that the tale went on – and on – with nothing much changing, for so long that the chroniclers fell into that mode that often signals time passing, when you hear the phrases 'They used to . . .' 'They were in the habit of . . .', 'They would go (come, do, say, agree to . . .)', those phrases signifying continuous thought or behaviour. And I, like other historians, have concurred that so much time did pass that generations of chroniclers, of Memories, died out and for some reason the attempt was not made to restart the process of activating Communal Memory.

But we were wrong, for there was an interruption to the lives of the two communities so severe that the comfortable and unremarkable development of them both stopped.

In both the histories the first mention of the catastrophe was the word 'Noise': 'When the Noise began . . .', 'The Noise went on . . .', 'We did not know what caused the Noise and some of us even went mad . . .'

The 'Noise' was in fact a wind, coming from what must have been the east, one so strong, so irresistible, that they all believed at first in all kinds of super-natural intervention.

Before arriving at the Clefts' shore, or even at the boys' valley, this wind had to tear its way from one end of the island to the other, bringing down whole forests, and whipping up the sea into furies of destruc-tion. The wind moaned and shrieked, it sobbed and it screamed, it was the Noise, something none of the people had ever imagined. Wind they had all known all their lives, the brisk spray off waves, the swaying and soughing of branches, but this? This Noise? And we, so long afterwards, have still to ask, what was it? What causes a wind so comprehensive that it lays flat the great forests and topples rocks off mountains, raises clouds of poisonous dust and goes on and on, moaning and screaming – and we do not know for how long. We have all, I think, lived through big storms, perhaps have even seen trees brought crashing down. What in nature could create a wind like the Noise that engulfed that island?

The boys in their flimsy shelters by the forest's edge found themselves helpless as the wind tossed them over and over, or threw them into the river. They could not find any place in their lovely valley where they could be safe. Up on the mountain no eagles could fly – most were killed or hurt in those long days and nights of the Noise. The boys crept up the mountain, keeping as low as they could to the ground, and went over the top, among the smashed eagles' nests and hurt birds, and found their way to the caves above the shore where the girls welcomed them, being glad of their presence. They were all distraught with fear and with knowledge of their helplessness. They did not have – or we believe they did not have – a personification for this wind, the Noise, they did not pray – I believe – to wind's being. They all, including the ones who seldom left the shoreline, got as far into the caves as they could and wept and trembled together. There is no mention at all of the Old Shes, the Old Females, and from this we have agreed to believe that they had died out, and that none of the young ones had grown into the status and stature of the Old Ones. Those caves above the sea were full, crowded with people, all hungry and afraid. They could not go out into the storm to catch fish, and could not light their fires. The Noise went on, and went on, while it seemed as if the whole island would be lifted into the air.

What could have caused such a wind? Where was it blowing from? The chronicles did not immediately begin again, but when they did, it was said that any babes born were precious, guarded, and every baby was allotted to an older person, watcher or carer. The depletion of both the communities was such that there was speculation by the Memories that it would take very little to wipe out all the people living on the shores and the valley. A big storm – or Noise – could do it. 'There are so few of us,' the Memories had been instructed to keep in their records, perhaps as a reminder.

From the time of the Noise – the great wind – there was a new note in the histories of both shore and valley: the wind put fear into people who before had not – so it seems – known fear. They were apprehensive. The suddenness and surprise of the Noise changed them all. Of course bad things had happened

before, a death, a drowning, the unfortunate beginnings of the males, but when had a murderous attack
from Nature, surely their friend, happened before?
'What has happened may happen again.' The Noise,
the wind had taught them all how helpless they were.

The boys went back to their valley as soon as they
could. It is recorded that they could not stand the
supervision and the regime of the women. And they
felt unappreciated too. When the Noise was at its
height, and no one had eaten for days – weeks, perhaps
– the boys crept on their bellies down to the shore
to collect the fishes flung up by the violence of the
waves. They built great fires in empty caves and
cooked the fish. Some animals running before the
wind arrived on the shore, frantic and fearful, and
the boys killed enough with their bows and arrows
to feed them all. The women did not seem to admire
them for this cleverness. And, as always, came the
complaints about the messy and smelly caves.

Back in their valley they did not find the ease they
had remembered.

The great forest, which had stood there always like
a promise of plenty, had been flattened in large areas
by the wind. It was hard now even to walk in it, the
fallen trunks and branches made some parts impen-
etrable. The animals had suffered, and so had the
birds. When the boys came down the mountain they
could hardly recognise their place. The shelters and

sheds had been thrown down by the wind, or taken over by animals trying to find shelter. The valley seemed full of dung and churned-up soil. A track came from the destroyed forest to the river's edge where the animals had come for water. The wind had blown the water everywhere, so around the river's edge were marshes, and reeds and grass poked up out of the shallow waves.

The boys did not return to the caves, but tried to set their camp to rights. When they took a fish to the eagles' place no eagles came at once. They were pleased to be given food – the Noise had left some crippled, with broken wings and legs. The boys who could never be afraid of these great birds tried to help them, and even sent a message to the caves, asking for someone good at healing to come. From this time the eagles saw the females as friends, like the boys.

And from that time began the concern over the children, both Clefts and Squirts – but perhaps this is the moment to repeat a fragment of history. 'The rumour that when the first males were born they were called Monsters and were sometimes badly treated, even killed, must be considered as just that – rumour. A tale expressing some kind of deep psychological truth. It is now believed that the earliest ancestors were male, and if it is asked how they reproduced themselves, then the reply is that the eagles hatched them out of their eggs. After all, it cannot be for nothing that respect for the great birds is expressed in a hundred myths about our origins. It is much easier to believe that eagles, or even deer, were our progenitors, than that the people were in their beginnings entirely female, and the males a later achievement. After all, why do males have breasts and nipples if not that once they were of practical use? They could have given birth from their navels. There are many possibilities, all more credible than that females came first. And there is something inherently implausible about males as subsidiary arrivals: it is evident that males are by nature and designed by Nature to be first.'

This fragment certainly belongs to a much later time than anything else we have. It is from our histories – the males'.

There is a consistent theme in all the records after the Noise, the knowledge of a threat, a danger, inherent and unavoidable, and the concomitant: fear for the babies and small children.

The time had long gone when small boys had to fear attack from some of the females. When a little Monster was born there was no urgency about taking him over to the valley to be brought up there. From their first beginnings the boys had proved they could look after the babies – it was they who taught the deer to feed the babes and it was the older boys who were responsible for them. Boys sometimes guarded the little Clefts, too: often a small girl, or even an older one, taken to the valley when it was time for her mother to mate, begged to be left there. The children, boys and girls, enjoyed the valley, just as some preferred to live by the sea.

They were indulged, watched over and precious, both boys and girls.

Long ago the females had relinquished their capacity to become impregnated by a fertilising wind, or a wave that carried fertility in its substance; they did not become impregnated at all, except by the males. It took some time for this to be seen, by both males and females. There must have been a point when this knowledge went home, and probably painfully: the females had to be reliant on the males to get children. Did that mean both understood the means by which babes came to be lodged in female wombs? Did notions about fertilising winds and waves continue in the general consciousness but then – suddenly the truth was known? When the females lost their power to become pregnant, that must have been a relinquishing of belief in themselves, and how could that not have been painful? I am inclined to believe that the truth came home to both parties all at once, or at least within reasonable time. After all, from the start of this record (which purports to be representing both) sudden arrivals of knowledge, of understanding, were common, were how Nature managed its economies. Suddenly one, or two, or more individuals were different, thought differently, obeyed impulses that were new to them. So, it seems to me, the knowledge that it was the monstrous (once) arrangements of the males that put infants into the females happened all at once. Suddenly the truth was evident.

Together with the constant fretting and perturbation about the fewness of the children, and how vulnerable they all were, went – in the tales of the males, and of us – complaints about the females' continual nagging at them. The females found the males lacking, and we have now perhaps to wonder if this expressed a deeper dissatisfaction – because females were so fundamentally dependent on the males.

And while all this went on an older pattern (we may call it a preNoise pattern) also went on.

All the babies were born in the caves above the sea, and they played in the waves and were safe. Most females lived in the caves, because they did not like the valley, and most males lived in their valley. There was constant visiting. The girls went to the valley when they had to, and the males sometimes spent time in the caves. New little males were not brought up by the men, but were with the little girls. The caves, full of little children, boy-babes and girl-babes, would not look so very different from a collection of our children. The children, the girls and boys, often went to the valley. The valley was a wondrous and amazing place, for both the little girls and little boys.

The women did not like the children to be in the valley – and here is sounded another consistent complaint from them. The great river, recovered from the Noise, ran as swiftly and as strongly as ever, and the children were at risk. The newly built sheds and shelters were as dirty and unkempt as ever and, if the children enjoyed that, the women complained and tried to keep the children with them on the shore. But that changed because it became the custom for the little boys to leave their mothers and the caves, and join the men, when they were about seven. In language not unfamiliar to us now, the boys described the caves, and the seashore, and their mothers as soft and babyish. The big river and its dangers were seen as initiatory, and desirable for the boys' development. Soon all the boys had to leave the caves and learn to dare the dangers of the cold, deep, deadly river currents. When one, and then another, died the males seemed to think this a reasonable risk.

 Some events this summer make me resume my comments.

I preface what I have to say with the reminder that the Spartans removed boy children from their mothers at the age of seven.

Titus and I had ridden out to our estate early in

the summer, expecting not to see Julia and Lydia till early autumn. But Julia sent me a message that she meant to go to a wedding party on the farm next to ours and would drop in. The new husband was Decimus, and Julia had been his mistress for years. Decimus was marrying ambitiously, Lavonia, a highly placed girl. Decimus sent a chariot to bring Julia to the wedding, and one afternoon this pretty vehicle, garlanded and beribboned, arrived with Lydia as well as Julia. The women got out and I went out to greet them. Titus saw them and was running up but then, really seeing his mother and his sister, stopped, and stood frowning at them: the sun was in his eyes. But that was not the trouble: Julia and Lydia made a dazzling pair. Julia wore a rose-coloured gown, and the little girl a light mauve one, designed for her by her mother. What a handsome woman Julia was now, and the girl, an apparently frail and delicate little thing, set her off. Julia saw a good-looking boy, staring at her. She did not at once know this was her son, whom she had scarcely seen for a year or so. Her first reaction was to flirt, send him smiles that acknowledged his attractions, but this impulse was cut off as she took in his pose. He had half turned away, hands loose, his body saying that he was about to take off and away.

Next to his mother his sister stood smiling. 'Look at me! Just look at me. You almost didn't recognise me, did you?' Those two had been good friends always, until the summer before, when Lydia seemed almost overnight to enter into some ancient endowment – a newly arrived sexual knowledge, an instinctual understanding of herself and of the male sex. Her smiles at her brother were not acknowledging their friendship, but that she was an adult and he must recognise that. Is there a greater gulf than between a thirteen-year-old boy and his fifteen-year-old sister, already a woman? My boy was stunned, as if the smiles of the two women had been poison-tipped arrows. He could not move.

Meanwhile Julia was equally immobilised. This was her son, this beautiful boy. She did not know how to behave. Then she took a step towards him and ruffled her hand through his hair – a beautiful white hand where shone my first wife's rings, and my mother's. The boy took a step back, frowning. He was as tall as she was. His eyes, on a level with her wonderful dark eyes, stared, stern, grave – accusing? Certainly he repudiated her and her silly caress. I believe that she was feeling, as I had so many years ago, that this was her son and she had lost all the years when she could have known him. I don't know: she never said so, but she was certainly penitent, standing there. Her eyes filled with tears. Meanwhile, just behind her, the chariot's horse was stamping and tossing his head: the reins were too tight. I signalled to the charioteer to loosen the horse's head, and I saw that Julia at the same moment had seen the discomfort of the horse, and that she might have remedied things herself. She was overcome with

shame, a complex of regrets, standing there, this beautiful woman, in the hot sunlight. The slave with the
sunshade was holding it steady, but the sun was
striking Julia's cheek.

I have always said that she has a good heart, she is
a kind woman. I think her present associates would
laugh to hear me say so. They know the woman who
screams applause at the blood in the arena, the death
throes of the animals, and of the gladiators. Yet that
afternoon she felt for that mistreated horse.

She was such a picture of vulnerability – helplessness? – and I impulsively did something that I had
planned to say to her, alone.

I believed she was mistaken, agreeing to go to this
wedding, particularly when the new husband had made
a point of sending a very elegant little chariot. Julia
would shine at this wedding, no matter how many
other pretty women would be there. I stepped forward,
and put my arms around her and whispered into her
ear just visible under one of the monstrously compli-
cated coiffures that are fashionable now, 'Be careful,
little partridge, be careful, Julia.'

Lydia heard these words. I do not believe that either
of the children had seen many tender moments between
their parents. Julia, careful not to disturb her compli-
cated tresses, responded by melting into my embrace
(I have to say, like a daughter, rather than a wife) and
she whispered, 'Thank you, my dear, thank you –
always.' Her daughter's eyes flashed – jealousy, that so
primeval emotion, mother-and-daughter jealousy. Lydia

even put out her hand as if to pull her mother away from me, but let it drop. Meanwhile the boy stood, staring at us. If we had been in private I would have gone on, 'It is not unknown, Julia, for a new wife to punish her predecessor or even try to kill her.' But I could see Julia was thinking hard, as she deftly let me go, patting her rolling black locks.

(In the event Lavonia, the new wife, died in child-birth in the spring of the following year.)

Tears flowing on her pink cheeks, Julia stepped into the chariot, and Lydia, obviously feeling that she had not made enough of a statement, came to embrace me. This was not false, we had always got on well, little Lydia and I – but little Lydia was not here this after-noon, here was this lovely young woman, returned to being a child for a moment. Then, feeling herself as she had been so recently as a few months ago, she went towards her brother, not coquettishly, or flirta-tiously, but sending him glances like a friend – like a loved sister. But Titus had turned away from her. Lydia, spurned, tossed her head and was ready to sulk, but then she too got into the chariot and off they went, the two women, to the next estate. It was only a short distance: they could have walked it easily.

And I stood there in the wonderful afternoon, eagles wheeling overhead, sparrows chirping from a near bush.

The boy turned from the women in a violent impulse of escape and leaped, once, twice, more – he went running across the already sun-parched fields. And that was how I remember that summer – the boy in movement, in flight, by himself or with the herdsmen's boys, or the house slaves' sons. These had always played together, but what I was watching was not play.

The house servants, who of course had known Titus all of his life and could be said to be secondary mothers, loved him. Some had seen that little play by the chariot. They knew what it all meant – the slaves and servants know far more of us than we like to think. They wanted to make up to the boy for his careless mother, but tenderness was not what he needed then. Watching him in his strenuous activities, climbing high and dangerously in the hills where the eagles nested, running races with the other boys, high at the top of trees so tall I could hardly bear to watch, the somersaults, the acrobatics, the competitions they set up for themselves, I felt that he was trying to outrun something or somebody, to free himself. I was reminded of once when some slaves were sent to get fish from the marsh and the midges were out looking for food. The slaves were dancing and leaping about inside a dense cloud of the insects, swatting at their heads, their arms, their legs.

You could imagine that an invisible cloying clinging substance was attacking my boy, and he was trying to free himself.

He became gaunt and lean, that summer, no longer a child, but a strong youth, even a man.

He refused to see his sister, and was not at home when Julia arrived, ready to see him.

This summer made me think of my childhood. I was

one of three brothers, older than the little girl, born late in my mother's reproductive life. We boys petted the girl, made her our plaything – and ignored her when she got in the way of our games. How hard it can be for a boy younger than a loved sister, I saw that summer.

I tried to be always available for him, tried to show – silently – how I felt for him. And so did the servants and slaves – the women. He was a polite boy, good-hearted, he did not repel them, fend them off – but he fled from them, his face always averted from them.

One afternoon I had picked a little bunch of flowers, and I was walking down towards our statue of Artemis, in a grove where paths crossed, when I saw Titus walking behind me, looking to see what I was doing. I beckoned to him and he nodded, but stayed behind me, his steps audible on the hard late-season earth. When I was a boy (like my father), I loved Diana, the tomboyish girl, whom I thought of as a playmate, who understood me. I left her little gifts and hoped that one day I would come on her, with her girls, and she would recognise me. Later I found her too young for me and loved Artemis. When I reached the statue, I bowed and set the little bunch of flowers at her feet. I hoped Titus would see me and understand what I felt. I could not say to him, your mother, your sister are not the only representatives of the female sex.

He was standing close to me, looking with me at the beautiful Artemis. I was silently saying to him, no matter how hard things get, we can always rely on something that will never change. Smiling, beneficent Artemis will be here for ever. It is not possible to imagine that she could ever be absent. I have never felt much for Juno, Minerva, Hera, they are too far from me. They, too, will always be in their heavens. But Artemis – I feel as close to her as to my mother, or my poor first wife. So you see, Titus, remember: she is here, and she will always be here, her statue will stand here, smiling, for always.

Life on the river changed with time. Boats arrived, some not more than trunks of trees, or bundles of reeds. There were festivals at the river, where all the females came to take part, and there was dancing and feasting. Festivals, which have about them a sense of 'We always do it this way', cannot be imagined during the very earliest days of the people. Now there were feasts, where fire played such a part, the cooking of flesh killed in the forest – we are talking about an age, or ages, passing.

By now the young of these people, both males and females, regularly met at the Killing Rock, which had long ago forgotten its horrid history, and there were races and wrestling and all kinds of acrobatics. It is not possible to imagine the soft, fat, slow females of the earliest times wrestling or even running. I think we must assume their physique had changed, the strong, muscled, fat-protected bodies of the girls who swam faster than they could ever walk had slimmed and become lithe and flexible.

Meanwhile – and what a long *while* that was – all the little boys clamoured to be part of the river life. They were not like our indulged boys always watched over by their slaves, perhaps earning indulgent smiles as they played soldiers and the miniature legionnaires tested their strengths. These children from infancy had known their way over the mountain. No use for Maire or her successors saying, 'We do not allow it.' How could they reinforce their prohibitions? Fearless little boys, some not much more than infants, found their way to the valley, and the women could chide and rebuke as much as they liked.

Things were always easier in the valley. Now there were equal numbers of Clefts and Squirts – we have to deduce this – the boys were delivered of their constant restlessness and need, whose causes they did not understand. Not that we can now say what they understood and what they did not. How do we now look at the word 'understand'? One thing to say, 'We know that the Clefts come to us and we play our games and then later they produce babies.' Yes, but that is very far from what we believe the girls thought. They had to know that without 'the games' they played with the boys, there would be no babies. During the time of the great wind, the Noise, little mating went on, and the Clefts had to notice, if the boys did not, that there were no babies being born when it was reasonable to expect babies. Did they say 'nine months' or anything like that? We do not know. But they knew there was an interval after mating and then there was a baby, girl or boy.

Just as there were continual complaints by the Clefts about the dangers the little boys were expected to face, so there were complaints from the Clefts, specifically about the great river. The little boys should not be allowed to go near the river, said the women.

Oh, how the females hated that river valley. That comes clear and insistent from the chronicles and songs of the time. Most of all they hated the river itself, which was dangerous to them, not only to the infants and small children. The theme 'How few we are, how easily we die' – the words of a song – is reiterated. Many had died in that river.

It ran very fast, it was deep, it was cold, and to bathe in it they all, except for the strongest of the young men, had to confine themselves to a bay or inlet where water idled and lazed, and it was shallow. These people who had been born on the edge of the sea, had always been in and out of the water, who had felt about water almost as they did about air, benign, safe, their element, now knew water as an enemy. On the insistence of the Clefts, there were guards on the river banks, preventing the small children from going in. The bigger boys willingly did this. They were as handy with the small children as were the females. Had they not nurtured many of their own, with the eagles' help? Had they not taught deer to feed the babes? It was not that they didn't know how to look after small children, they were rather too casual, the females complained; the boys were forgetful. The older boys would start a game with some tiny boy who was trying to reach the enticing water, but the game became general, with the other little boys coming in, and the first little one would be forgotten, or even knocked over and into the water. The females exhorted the boys, trying to teach them consistency of care. In the end, the guards on the river banks included females: they could not trust the boys to remember their duties.

The Clefts for the time believed that the boys were defective, mentally: they did not have normal memories. This idea developed to 'they are born normal but then later they don't seem to think of anything but their squirts'.

One of the games developed by the boys caused a violent altercation.

The more adventurous boys, and this did not necessarily mean the older ones, would step away from the safe bay, and fling themselves into the fast-running waves of the main river. They let themselves be carried along until they reached a certain little island further down the river. They clambered out, rested, and then had to reach the bank, a dangerous swim, where they ran back and jumped into the swimming shallows, and then again leaped into the cold and rapid waves. Sometimes, if a log or a branch was travelling along in the flow, they might catch it and hold on and use it for the ride. The females did not do this, that is to say, the older ones, though the younger Clefts joined in. What the Clefts objected to was allowing the young boys to join in. It was certainly very dangerous, and a little child did lose hold of his support and drowned.

There is mention of mourning for this child, very different in emphasis from the careless, even indifferent, attitude towards much earlier deaths. This child was valued. The dead infant was not consigned to the water, but brought back to the main bank from the little island where he had been caught on an underwater snag. The child was buried on the edge of the forest with stones over the place, to prevent the body being dug up by animals.

There is mention now, often, of the big animals that sometimes came out of the trees.

Apart from the dangerous river, great fires were kept burning always, day and night, because of these animals, who were afraid of fire, and the fires too had guards.

A new thing, now, the constant references to danger, to threat: 'How few we are, how easily we die.'

This is why we think now this period went on for

a long time: enough to develop new customs, feelings, ideas.

What did they feel when they buried that small child? What, when the Old Ones died? Did they put some fish near the infant's grave for his journey into the afterlife? Did they believe in an afterlife?

When this infant died, from the young men's carelessness – so the Clefts thought – the girls from the shore demanded a debate with the boys, insisted on decisions being made about safety.

The men suggested meeting on a certain stretch of shore. Before that there would be a feast. There was much excitement and enjoyment, 'games' went on most of the night, and a full moon surveyed the festivities. On that night it would have been easy to believe the moon had once filled the wombs of the Clefts, before the coming of the boys. Not many slept, and when the sun came up the girls were still trying to entice the boys into more 'games'. There was ill feeling when the boys said now it was time to go off to the shore they had designated for their deliberations. In fact there were none for the boys were only interested in their pastime, which on that day was well favoured, because high tide had exposed even more of the stones they needed for a certain sport. The girls' description of the day was irritated, exasperated, but the boys' account only said the girls 'were complaining as usual'.

This is what happened.

This seashore, unlike the rocky shore the females knew so well, was a long edge of white sand, and on this were stones, all smoothed by the sea, pleasant to handle – and the females were doing that, playing with them, and wondering how to attach them to make necklaces and adornments from them.

Meanwhile the men were standing where the waves stopped, and throwing the stones with a low skimming motion over the waves and making them skip once, twice, three times, until the stones sliced into the waves. 'What are you doing?' said the women, and the men said, 'These are the best conditions we've had,' and, 'If you don't mind, we aren't going to waste them.' 'Yes, but we are here to talk about safeguarding the little boys.' 'Well, wait, then.'

But on they went, throwing the stones, admiring each other's skills, while the women were at first puzzled, then astounded, then affronted. 'What's the point?' the women asked each other. 'What are they doing?' 'Perhaps they want us to admire them.' The men were naked, except for their little aprons of feathers. They were certainly a challenge, an invitation, as some girls saw it, and they tried to entice the boys away from their game to play with them. But the boys did not seem to feel they were trying to make the girls admire them, so absorbed were they in their stone-throwing. 'Three . . . four . . . five . . .'

said a boy. 'But I did six,' said another. 'No, you didn't, that was five.' So they bantered, competing over the skipping stones, matching their skills and ease with the stones. Surely they would soon be bored? was what the women were thinking. 'What's the point of doing this? *What do they think they are doing?*' But the men just went on. It was warm and then it was hot. The sun hit straight down from the burning sky. The females retreated to patches of shade, where they sat, arms round their legs, watching. What skill was going into the men's game, and what concentration. And what was it all for? was the thought exchanged between the women in their unhappy glances. It was midday and time, surely, to find shade, find even a cave perhaps, and sleep, or play, as the women wanted. Then the men, as if at a signal, stopped their game and began another. The tide was going out, exposing the tops of weed-slippery black rocks. The men, all of them, down to the little boys, were jumping from rock to rock in daring leaps which, though apparently impossible, mostly succeeded. If they fell into the sea, and even cut themselves, they had to continue the game bleeding. On they went to see who could jump further, jump furthest, faster, more skilfully.

A little boy cut his knee and came to the women to have it bound with seaweed and then he at once returned to the others.

The women made a point of showing the bleeding child to the men, who did not seem to find it any proof of their negligence, but indicated by their manner that the women were – as usual – absurd.

A group of youths wandered off, not greeting the women or even seeming to see them. The light went out of the sky and the women looked to see the youths return but the others said they were a hunting party and probably wouldn't get back that night. Often hunters stayed at a good place to take advantage of the early morning when animals emerged from the trees to go down to the waterholes and streams.

There was no suggestion that the promised discussion would take place: the incident with the damaged little boy had to do in place of the reproaches the women had planned.

That night there was no feasting. There was some mating but nothing like last night, though the moon stood there above them.

In the early morning the women woke to find there was not one male to be seen. Hard to avoid the thought that the men had seen the women, their females, asleep and silent, and stolen off silently, so as to – escape? Yes, almost certainly, that was what they had done.

The women decided to give up. They went back along the shore to their own place, sad, disappointed and feeling let down, although later some of the hunting party brought them a carcass and arranged the parts to cook around a fire. It seemed they felt they were apologising.

Something like this happened more than once, and the comments entrusted to the Memories included remarks about the men's mental equipment. Speculation went on. Were they mad? Hard to see a whole day's skimming stones over the waves as a sane activity. No, they were – at least sometimes – crazy. Perhaps the full moon affected them? After all, if the full moon regulated the women's fertility and their menses, then the full moon could wreak otherwise sane minds into lunacy. It was generally agreed in the end that the men were, if not mad, then deficient in understanding.

Yet there were some girls who refused to leave the men's valley, and said they liked the life there. Then, first one and then another, they returned, angry and fearful, because they were pregnant, and as their bellies swelled were told they were not wanted, even though they were useful, cutting up carcasses, making fire, clearing away rubbish and the remains of feasts. 'Back to your own place,' they had been told, though some did not want to go. The women's shore, with so many pregnant females, babies, small children, was not peaceful, though there was plenty of entertainment for the babes and infants, in and out of the waves, water babies, like the young of seabirds or like sea pups. The cold slapping and slicing waves could never lose their allure for the adults.

But the contrast between the women's shore and the men's valley was hard for some females, hard to bear.

It was not that the men did not come to visit the women in their airy caves, or that the women did not go to see the men.

Then occurred the confrontation which sent the males out of their valley into the forests.

The young men were always inventing for themselves daring feats and challenges, and they came up with something that sent Maronna, 'half mad with rage', over the mountain to Horsa. Maronna, the name appears about now, and so does Horsa. We do not know if the syllables with Mar . . . Maro . . . Mer and similar represented an individual or, as we think, the current leader of the women.

The youths went together with forest rope – the underside of the bark of trees – to The Cleft, and one of their number tied rope round his middle, and jumped down on the platform where the fumes from the ossuary below soon overcame him. The game was that those standing on the rim, peering down, had to haul him up before he passed out. They all did this, one after the other; those who had never attempted The Cleft were not considered adult.

Maronna went alone, and found Horsa just off into the forest to hunt.

Our chronicle says Maronna physically attacked Horsa and had to be restrained. Their chronicle says Horsa apparently did not know he was at fault in anything, until she screamed at him that he never thought about his actions, never saw consequences . . . everybody knew that the little boys emulated the big boys in anything, and when they attempted to jump down to the platform, first, they would be using seaweed rope which almost certainly would not be enough to hold them, and also, they were children, and not strong enough either to withstand the fumes at all, or, if handling the 'rope', would not prevent themselves from being tugged over and into the gulf.

'Are you trying to kill off all our children?' shouted Maronna, and Horsa, who had never thought until this moment that the small boys would of course try to follow the example of the big youths, shouted that there was no need for her to shout and scream, he would make sure the practice stopped at once.

Did Horsa apologise, admit he had been thoughtless? – because of course she was right. I cannot see Horsa ever admitted he had been in the wrong, but our chronicle says that Maronna was 'pacified' and he agreed to put a guard at The Cleft, day and night, to make sure no little boys went up there.

'Don't you care about us?' Maronna demanded, weeping.

This has earned the scrutiny of a hundred commentators. What did she mean by 'us'? The appellation 'the people' seems to have been dropped long ago. Did she mean that the males did not care about the trials of the women? Or about the little boys? ('Very few of the girls were tempted by the trial by fumes – they said it was sacrilegious, and The Cleft was holy.' This kind of talk was not often recorded, about the Clefts, and we have to think, then, that they were inventing religious reasons to criticise the boys.)

Did these people, women and men, have an idea of themselves as the only people alive, as suggested by the song, 'How few we are, how easily we die'? There is no record anywhere, either by them or by us, that they believed there were other people like themselves or even unlike themselves somewhere else 'on another island'. It seemed they believed this land of theirs was an island, though I wonder what they thought an island was. An island or land implies other islands or lands and we shall see that Horsa would soon go off in search of other shores, if not other people.

We return to what did she mean by 'us'? There is certainly a suggestion there of the consciousness of a threat, or several.

This question did reach Horsa, and it is recorded that he thought about it. There was a good deal to think about: for two at least of his young men had succumbed to the effluvias of The Cleft, and fallen into its depths. More than one small boy had drowned in the great river. Going off into the forest was as much a safety measure as it was a need to avoid the continual criticism from Maronna.

Horsa was a young man with remarkable capacities, and his name dominates this part of our story. There was a constellation they called Horsa, and when we think how names began, sometimes we may easily hear the snarl of a wolf, the growl of a bear. Horsa's animal familiar was a stag, so we may entertain ourselves thinking that the bark of a deer became Horsa, the name of the famous hunter.

When the women went to the valley as usual, the men were gone. The ashes of the great fire were cold. The eagles were not sitting in their places like tutelary gods, and the bits of fish and bones had been scattered by animals.

As they stood around, wandered about, dismayed, even desperate, an eagle did come floating down and settled in its place. 'Well, where are they? Don't you see? We have to find them.' The bird did not seem to wish them ill but made no attempt to show them where the men had gone, and soon it rose up and flapped its way slowly up and back to the eyries on the mountain top.

The young females said they would go and look

for the men, who were, it was pretty certain, not far along the shore. Unlikely the boys would leave the shore for the interior, but this was their own preferences speaking – the women's. There was another reason the men could not be far: the little boys living here in the valley had gone with the men and that surely meant they must all be close. The older females said they would wait at the river's edge for a few days, and watched as the young ones set off along the shore looking for the fires which would mean the men were there.

And yes, they found they looked down from cliffy heights on to a beach where the men were, and the boys – all the males – who, seeing the women, let out cries of welcome and pleasure, mingled, however, with sounds of – derision? Yes. The girls who reported this arrival told too that they were upset at the criticism, and it was not the only time jeers at the women greeted their arrival. To me – to this male, even so very long after – it was pretty clear what was happening. The females were associated, for the boys, with criticism and complaint – and I must record, perhaps as a small and I hope not inept addition to the history, that it is always a little humorous when nagging changes, without much warning, into a plea for – well, as soon as the women clambered down the cliffs to the white sands, there were multiple matings and encounters in and out of the surf. The young boys stood around watching, and perhaps trying out ideas of their own on each other, as we may see animals do.

This was daytime, and towards night hunting parties returned from the trees with carcasses, which were cut up and there was much sex.

The women had been ready to criticise the men for taking the little boys along with them on this expedition, but about one thing the women had been wrong. These boys, some of them as young as six and seven, were in no way babies, or infants, nor needed concessions to their smallness in the way of running or climbing.

The men did not treat the little boys in any way differently from themselves and the women had to acknowledge that these small boys were as hardy and speedy as the men. This acknowledgement meant that later, when the little boys were so anxious to go off and live with the men, the women's anxiety was lessened.

The older females came along in a day or two, and there was a considerable and lengthy meeting, full of festivity and many games.

Then the women returned to their shore and the men went into the forest.

We have here to acknowledge a good long time, an age – how long? – when there were groups of the males in various parts of the forest, where there were suitable rivers or inviting glades. And women went to visit them, when their nature told them it was time. And now it was evident that we are talking about sizeable populations – quite a few females on their shore, and some males in their valley. So, how many? There is no way of calculating, particularly when it is known that among the men were always girls, who were not merely the visiting females, but who had decided that they preferred the men for company. These females were for some reason not fertile or had made sure they were not, or were sterile, and this meant they did not discommode the men with their babes. We know that some deliberately got rid of their babes when they were born. And who are we Romans to criticise, who at so much later a time do the same, leaving unwanted infants out on hillsides to their fate? There is one fact shown by this: that these people were no longer afraid that they were too few. 'How few we are, how easily we die.' Not any longer. The Noise was a long time in the past.

And it is a fortunate or unfortunate fact that we, the peoples of the world, are very fertile, fecund, forever proliferating. There are more babes born than are needed. It is Nature's way, is it not? She oversupplies, over-provides, always and in every-thing.

I think this is where we must face a certain question, even if it cannot be answered. Where was this island where our remote ancestors crawled (we think) out of the sea to become us? Of course, many have tried to establish which island and where. How large an island? Like Sicily? No, too small, surely. Perhaps Crete? But we know Crete has suffered earthquake and invasion by the sea. Someone brought the bundle of ancient writings here to Rome, from – one of the isles of Greece? The argument against this is the climate, for nowhere in the chronicles is mentioned burning suns and crackling heat and the bitter dusts of summers that drag on into drought. But all that could mean was that these people had never experienced anything different from what they knew, and did not think extremes worth recording – though they certainly recorded the Noise, the great storm. It was not a cold island: they never wore much more than wreaths of seaweed, or the men's feathers and leafy aprons. So they went naked, or almost. We may assume they were brown, since all the populations we knew about are a shade of brown or perhaps brownish yellow. If other colours of hair or eyes existed there was no reason for these people ever to know about it. They probably had brown eyes.

These whispers from the past, the immense past, voices that repeat what has been said by other voices, we have to interpret by what we know, what we have experienced – and our questions disappear as if they were stones dropped into a very deep well. After all, we Romans did not always know that to our north were populations with corn-coloured hair and blue or grey eyes.

Suppose the climate of that long ago has changed so that we have no means of knowing what it once was? Balmy and beneficent shores where lived people through long ages, slowly evolving from – but we do not know – to . . . We do know they called themselves the people as if there could be no others in the world. But that is the common tale of the beginnings of a people.

In our (comparatively) recent times it is happening that old Greece, once thickly forested, is becoming bare rocky hillsides. How do we know that the blessed land of that ancient people is not now all rocky arid outcrops – and not further away than our sailors may travel.

At the point our tale has reached, there were several communities separate from each other, not on the sea's edge, but in the interior in the forests, always near streams and rivers. They sometimes fought. Over what? Certainly not food – the forests were full of food. No, it was space. Large parts of the forest were swamp, marsh, and that was because the Noise, that great storm, had felled trees as easily as one of our breaths may blow seeds off a stalk. Old rotting trunks in unhealthy water – and so it was that there was not enough of the desirable forest for everyone. And again there is a reminder here that these are not small groups we are talking about, but a serious number of people.

The leaders of the different communities sometimes fought, and there were casualties, and the women sent protests and admonitions – but it was Horsa who ended the fighting. We know about him that he was brave and a good leader, but perhaps there were many Horsas, one after the other supplanting each other, and Horsa was simply the name for the main leader.

Meanwhile, over on the female shore Maronna ruled, not in the sleepy way of the Old Females, but with vigour and – it is suggested – often impatiently. Certainly this Maronna made her way past the marshes and the swamps to the part of the forest where Horsa ruled and it was because of her chiding that the fighting ended. There are suggestions that the men enjoyed the fighting, pitting their wits against each other. When there were wounded, they were taken to the women's shore to mend.

Before Horsa went off on his trip, there was a bad quarrel between Horsa and Maronna. Earlier chronicles said that this was one event, referred to as the Men's Rage, the Women's Rage, depending on the gender of the speaker. Rage there was, but it was misreported, misunderstood, as a single defining confrontation. I remember the satisfaction, the feeling – and there is nothing like it for an historian, that moment when I realised the truth – that there might have been a culmination of disagreements in rows neither side could easily forgive and forget. There had been successive complaints from both, and all the differing versions described the same thing, unnecessary multiplications of the 'Rage'. 'Of course, how was it I didn't see that before' – and it is seldom enough insights come so clearly and cleanly, to add up to a conviction. One trouble is that the men's version is so brief. As usual, when Maronna came, having sent us complaints by the visiting girls, she always said the same things. And the girls' messages were the same, the men were irresponsible, thoughtless, careless of our lives and particularly about the boys' safety. We took it for granted that what we spoiled, the women would put right. That really was all there was to the men's version. 'And so Horsa decided to go away, to find some place far enough from Maronna to make it impossible for her easily to come after us.'

This is to the point, I think:

I was walking a few days ago with Felix, my slave, who made the lovely statues of Diana and Artemis, and on a certain slope of a hill I remarked that I had often thought what a good site this would be for a house. Yes, we have a fine house on the estate but I enjoy thinking about an even finer one.

We paced around a bit, argued that this place would be better than that – and no more was said. Today Julia arrived without warning at the town house, and she said there was urgent news. I could see from her face it would be better if we were not overheard – Lolla was tidying the next room. I put my hand on Julia's arm and drew her out to the courtyard, and there she said, 'This is serious, where can we talk?' We knew Lolla would be listening if she could, and there was an old slave sitting by the wall. I walked with her to the fig tree, and we could see nobody else who might listen.

'You mustn't do it, my dear, everyone is talking about your new house, it is just madness even to think of it.' I was admiring my lovely wife, while noting that I never had heard her so peremptory, so harsh. Julia is ever charming, does not go in for scoldings. 'But Julia, how can "everyone" be talking? I hardly know myself – I just mentioned the possibility to Felix, that's all.' She stood, checked, her eyes searching my face, not doubting me, but puzzled. I was ready to pooh-pooh the whole rumour, but then exclaimed, 'Wait, yes, I understand.' My father freed two of his favourite slaves. One sells tripe near the docks, the other meat pies not far from the gladiators' quarter. Both are friendly with our slaves. Felix had come to our town house a few days before, said that the Master was thinking of building a new house, and so the rumour had gone – and so quickly – from this house to: 'We all know about it, and believe me you aren't being very wise this time.' Julia's pet name for me is Father Wisdom, from the very first days of her coming to me.

I told her the basis of this rumour, how flimsy – and that I wasn't really planning to build this famous house, it was just a whim.

'A whim!' she exclaimed, and looking around her in case someone else had come into the courtyard, she came close to me, and put her arms round me – a wifely gesture, but its rarity would be bound to startle any watching slave into suspicions. Julia, her mouth very close to my ear, said, 'Listen to me, have you forgotten? You're such an old dreamer these days, perhaps you haven't really taken it in.' And she began whispering into my ear the names of prominent people who have had their houses, their estates, herds, silver or gold dishes, confiscated by our latest tyrant. 'Do you really want to lose this house to Nero?' she said, dropping her already low voice to not more than a breath of sound. 'Nero is worse, worse every day. Do you mean to say it never crossed your silly old head that if you started building some fine new house that would be like an invitation for him to take it?' Now she released me, and started adjusting my toga, and taking her silver comb from somewhere in her robe, she began tidying my hair. It had been a long time since I had stared from so close into my wife's face. I was looking to see if the fast, self-indulgent life she led was showing on those pretty features. There were tired lines round her eyes, not much more. 'When I heard them all talking last night, I knew I had to come and warn you,' she said, very low.

Who was 'them'? – but I had a pretty good idea. 'And are you being careful, Julia?' I whispered.

She nodded, and smiled. 'Thank you. Sometimes you are such a foolish old thing,' she whispered and actually shook me a little.

'But Julia,' I whispered, 'this house has no existence except in my head.'

'You had better tell Lolla that you thought of building the house but Felix said the spring has too little water in summer. No, wait, better still, you don't have enough funds to build now, you might think of it in a year or two.' And again she came close to whisper, 'He can't last for ever, can he?'

And now she stood away a few steps, and said loudly, 'There, you see, a good thing you have me to keep an eye on you. Look at that toga. I'll bring a new one next time I come.'

'I hope that will be soon,' I said and she laughed, a half-teasing, half-regretful laugh. I like to think my Julia is sometimes sorry I am too old for her. At least I must be a nice change from that raffish lot she runs around with. Arm in arm we went back to the house, where we could see Lolla's face at a window. Julia said loudly, 'Oh dear, what a pity you are short of money just when I was going to ask you for a big sum. Leptus has some houses he wants to sell. Oh, Lolla, there you are.' Louder still, she said, 'Your trouble is you don't see the consequences of your actions, my dear. I could have told you not to put your money into that ship going to Thessaly. It's sunk, didn't you know? It's sunk, lost all its cargo.' I went with her to the outer door where her chair was waiting, with its slaves. We smiled at each other, tender conspirators, and off the chair went. So my poverty would be gossip by nightfall. And I went to my study thinking that I hadn't ever heard from Julia before the exasperated tone of her whispers to me under the fig tree. Is that what she really thought of me, her Father Wisdom? I'm afraid I have to think so.

Maronna talked to Horsa as if he were a child – well, he could easily have been hers, after all. The women always talked down to the men, chiding and scolding. On one occasion, when Maronna arrived in the men's camp, very angry, it was because some small boys had been killed in the fighting, when the fighting still went on, and she, speaking for all the women, was pointing out that it was easy for them, the men, who never took on the boys when they were small, but always when they had stopped being demanding children, and the women had done all the hard work of rearing them, feeding, nurturing. It took a moment, said Maronna, to kill someone, and that moment ended years of painstaking, difficult hard work.

In our time our Roman matrons are committed to

publicly applauding the successes of their sons as soldiers. I have never heard anyone publicly make Maronna's complaint, that it takes years to breed up a boy to be fit for the legions, but they do sometimes say this kind of thing to their husbands – as I may affirm.

'So,' scolded Maronna, 'who has done all the hard work? Not you! You make sure you are a long way off when there are babes to tend and teach.'

And now I must fill in the background. When the boys were about seven, sometimes earlier, they made their way to find Horsa in the forests. This had been going on for so long that we may describe it as their custom. Between the shore and the forest settlement was a track that avoided swamp and marsh and mire, and was safe enough, provided no child was alone on it. The girls always travelled in groups and the little boys were exhorted that they must do the same. But there were many animals, and more than once an unaccompanied small boy was taken. Maronna demanded that Horsa should insist the boys leaving the women's shore should take off openly, so that they could be accompanied. Horsa and all the men laughed at her. That she should say this meant she had no understanding at all of the boys, their feelings – and, by extension, of the men's. Of course the boys needed to sneak away from that overcrowded shore full of small children and babes, of course, that was the whole point – if the boys' escape was going to be monitored by the women, the fun of the thing would be gone. 'Can't you see that?' demanded Horsa, and said that she was stupid.

The little boys – who felt themselves to be no longer little from that moment they crept from the women's shore, saw their escape as 'going to the trees'. There were few trees anywhere near the shore. It was a wonderful thing, to see the arrival of a batch of boys, who had had to evade the women trying to keep them a bit longer. When they saw the great clearing in the trees they were amazed at the munificence of it all – and at once were up in the trees. Forests covered the whole island – if it was one – except for the places where there was marsh and swamp. There was a practical advantage in taking to the trees: some predators could not climb, or not easily, into that great canopy of boughs and leaves. The boys were safer than the young males who lived mostly on the ground, or who went off on hunting trips.

There were reports that some groups of the men lived entirely in the trees, but this was not said of Horsa's people.

The boys, from seven or so, did spend most of their time up in the trees. What boy can resist the trees of a real forest? It was a good life. They came down to the ground to join in the meals, the feasting,

and trips. They made platforms in the trees, and
all kinds of pulleys and swings and walkways. The
life trained them in self-reliance and in physical
skills. There were of course accidents, and that was
another reason the women's complaints were so irritating. They said that when the boys fell and broke
a leg or an arm, the men sent them back to the
women's shore to be put right. Couldn't men at
least watch over the little boys enough to stop so
many falls – and even some deaths? This struck the
men as positively irrelevant. Of course boys will
venture into danger, and there must be accidents.
What was this extraordinary concern by the females
for safety?

Another confrontation between Maronna and
Horsa with anger, accusations, bitterness. There was
nothing the women could do. The boys, on reaching
the age of seven or even younger, were of course
going to run off to join the men.

All of the males had made the early journey, off
into the forest, every man had memories of the too-
crowded confined women's shore.

Horsa pointed out that there were many different
kinds of shore, none far away from the original one,
and there was no need for the females to stay where
they were. Yes, the caves were convenient, and the
men would confess to harbouring a fondness for them,
their earliest memories were lodged in the caves above

the sea. The cliffs everywhere were of soft sandstone and easily excavated. Horsa said that the men would make a new home for the women, every bit as good as what they had, and with much more space. But Horsa was up against a stubborn predilection for what they were used to, what they knew. 'Their' shore, said the women, was where every one of them, Clefts and males, had originated. And they weren't going to leave.

Maronna did not hear about Horsa's proposed expedition direct from him. It was the girls chatting among themselves that alerted her. Were they going along with Horsa? Perhaps for a short way? Maronna did not at once take in that the departure would be soon, until one of the girls asked if she, Maronna, would go? At last, and too late, she understood that several of the girls would go, and all the little boys currently with Horsa would go too. When she thought about the implications of this she was horrified. She did not at once take in that Horsa had not thought about these implications. Planning for a long term was certainly not his talent, but to mention just one of the problems: if the girls went along they would be pregnant, and then they would be a burden to the travellers. This was why at first Maronna believed that Horsa planned a short trip.

Then, some girls went up to the mountain top to

see if any men were in the valley and saw that down there, by the river, some youths were catching fish to make a feast for the eagles, to ask for their protection on their journey.

Some girls at once went down to join in. Some had never seen the great birds so close. Some children were frightened. But the boys were not at all afraid and piled up the fish, and sang to the birds as they ate.

> 'We are the children of the eagle
> You are our fathers.'

There were many eagle songs, some saying that the first of us had been hatched from eagles' eggs.

Well, eagles still hold the imaginations of us Romans. There is an eagle's nest on a rocky outcrop on my country estate and some of my slaves take food as offerings to the place. There is something in me that applauds this gift, as if it were due.

Our feeling for eagles must have originated somewhere. In saying this, am I claiming kinship with those ancient long-ago ancestors of ours? Are we 'children of the eagle' more than we know? I do know that when our Roman eagles go past with the legions I have to conceal my tears.

When the girls and children returned to the shore, and Maronna heard about the eagles' feast, she understood that this venture of Horsa's was a more serious thing than she had realised. At once she called to some girls to go with her, because the little boys had heard that Horsa was leaving his forest clearing and there would be nowhere for them to go running to when they wished to leave the women's shore. Besides, it was not fair that Horsa was taking some boys – not all much older than the little boys – who would be left behind. They intended to take up residence in the forest and wait for Horsa to return.

Off the little boys ran, with the girls and Maronna after them. Tough little boys, they were, made strong by swimming, and the girls were strong too. How many boys went off that day? 'A good many little boys' is all that we have. They hoped they would be in time to join the men, they all had heard about the trees that would be waiting for them.

A great space in the forest full of men and boys and youths was not what they saw when they arrived there. The trees stood, so many, so tall, so powerful, as if watching them. And there was something more. The vacated sheds and shelters had been invaded, some knocked down. Large black beasts were rootling and grunting, tuskers, with teeth like sharpened knives. We know they were pigs, porkers, not unlike the ones we breed, but enormous, much bigger than any we have, and not soft and well-fed like ours, but lean and fast and dangerous. These little boys had not yet learned to climb, and hardly understood the danger they were in. The girls, horrified, immobile with terror, tried to draw the children to them, but in a moment the herd had charged, and two of the little boys had been carried off, back out of the horrid clearing. The pigs did not follow; they had two items for their feast. What they seemed to be saying, though, was, 'This is our place, keep out.'

What a surveillance had been kept on the men and boys in their clearing. At night the gleam of yellow and green eyes must have been as familiar to the feasters as were the flare of the bonfires.

There was not only this ferocious type of pig, but a kind of feline, very large, able to defeat a porker, or more, and we know there were many of these in the forest. There were also dogs, a type of dog in packs. All of these had at night, beyond the light of the flames, watched the goings-on in the clearing. Bears? We know there were bears.

Once again I have to intervene and it is because, while telling my tale of forests and beasts and wildness, I have been conscious that it is not possible for us to imagine what it must have been like for them living always at the edge of vast trees from which at any moment some terrifying animal may pounce or leap. For us late people, our imaginations do not stretch so far back. How long has it been since any Roman strolling in our woods has come on a bear, wolves, anything more threatening than a wild cat? My sons, fighting with the legions in those ferocious German forests, had to fear wild beasts that for us are only in legend. Our dangerous animals are behind bars. Plenty of those, yes. And we go to the games to get the thrill of seeing them. Yes, I do go to the games, usually with my sister Marcella, who will never miss an exciting event. She likes me to go with her, because that proves she is not the sensation lover I tell her she is. My being there, by her side, proves to her she is a sane and civilised person. It is not possible to sit there as the beasts are brought in to fight, or to attack their criminal victims without one's blood beating and the heart pounding. I've tried to sit beside her and remain unmoved. At some point you find yourself shouting, rising to your feet, calling out, and the smell of blood drives you wild. Why do I go? At first I went to try myself but I know now that I can never be any better than that blood-lusting screaming crowd. The thing is, not to go, and these days, when the thrills of scholarship are mine, I do not go unless Marcella persuades me. It is sickening, and how can one not say so? Many people do say so, and that the spectacles are cruel and make every spectator a participant in the most revolting barbarity. And yet, saying it, admitting it, they go.

I have wondered, and ask myself even more, reading

about these ancient people in their forests, if what we say about the games is all that may be said? There is an element of the barbarian in every one of us who enjoys the games in the arena. But when we scream as the blood bursts from the mouth of some lion, or leopard – or any of the endless supply of wild animals that fill our arenas, is there not perhaps something else there? I ask myself, is it revenge? For how long did our kind live in the forests side by side with leopards, boar, wolves, packs of dogs, at any moment their victims? They could not have taken a few steps into the trees without glimpsing some predator, some terrible enemy. How many of our ancestors died to provide meals for their enemies, the wild beasts? We have forgotten all that. Perhaps we have because it was so terrible, the way I think we do the very bad things that happen to us. That she wolf who nurtured our first Romans, that generous and loving creature – did we not invent her to compensate for the long history when wolves harried and hurt us? Just as I think eagles have in the idea of them something else, more than admiration for their pride and beauty – eagles took lambs from the flocks of people who depended on them for their food, eagles may snatch up a child, so I've heard, in the wilder parts of our empire. To propitiate eagles, who belong to Jove, is a precautionary thing, and when we shout as a lion falls dead, are we not compensating for times when lions and big cats might have, often did, feed us to their cubs?

In our arenas we sit in our safe rows, eating and drinking and watching while the great beasts are let in to meet their deaths, but once they meant death to us.

We are proud people, we Romans, and do not find it easy to admit weakness or fallibility, but perhaps our screams, our applause, admit it all for us. We are safe in our seats and the animals that may have been brought from Africa, from the eastern deserts, are at our mercy. None in those cages below and around the arenas will escape, every one will die as we watch – but very few spectators ever think that once we were at their mercy. When I think of how, in that forest where Horsa had his camp, watching over the little boys who learned how to be brave men, under the protection of him and his bands of youths, at night the eyes of man's terrible enemies, the animals, gleamed at them in the light from the great fires that were kept burning always to frighten them away, my blood literally does run cold. Have we forgotten those long ages when at any moment some beast could leap out from the undergrowth or drop from an overhead branch? When we scream in the arena, it is revenge that we are hearing. Or so I think when I put myself in the place of those long-ago people, savages we call them, our own kind, our ancestors – us. Only our legionnaires who have fought in the wildest places of our empire can begin to imagine what our ancestors felt, venturing into those old forests.

Now Maronna, some girls and some little boys ran until they saw the men on a large beach, already lighting fires for the evening.

The women arrived, screaming accusations at the

men who screamed at them. The men shouted that only idiot women would think of letting the little boys go to the forest clearing when there were no men to protect them. This was certainly disingenuous because Horsa and the other men all knew of the 'tradition' of the boys escaping the women. It could have been easy for Horsa to work out that the little boys would go running to the clearing the moment they knew Horsa was leaving. Why did Horsa not leave some youths behind to protect the boys? The truth was, Horsa was shaken: that animals patrolled and prowled his forest place of course he knew, how could any of them not know how many were there, hunting as they did through the trees, but that the big porkers had taken possession so soon after their departure, that was a shock.

The two little boys had been taken and eaten, and here were more little boys, frightened and clinging to the women.

The confrontation went on, while the fires flared all along the beach and the light went out of the sky.

We have versions of this scene, both from the men's and women's histories. Maronna is described as tall, as strong, with long hair she wore braided and piled on her head. This suggests she wanted to look taller.

We do not know what 'tall' meant to them. Perhaps Horsa, that great hunter, was a little lean man, not tall and strong – as we, I think, must be bound to imagine him, perhaps like one of our Praetorian Guards.

This is the only place in all our records where hair is mentioned. They might have red hair, for all we know, like some of the tribes of the Gauls. They might all have been redheads, or blond. Unlikely, I think. Black or dark hair and black or dark eyes – that is most likely.

It is recorded that Horsa was furious because of his own delinquency, which he was hearing about as Maronna screamed at him. He had no idea yet just how lacking in forethought he had been. He was arranging a big feast for her and the women, while the altercation went on.

Maronna was weeping with anger and frustration and humiliation, and she was tired: it was a good long way from the women's shore to this one. Maronna said she was going home now, and taking the girls – who obviously did not want to go but would rather stay here, guests of the men, with whom she was bitterly quarrelling. For one thing it was just coming home to her that Horsa was planning a long expedition. Horsa said none of the women could leave until morning: it would be dangerous, surely Maronna could see that?

She was trying to make him see certain things.

Have you thought that the girls going with you

will be pregnant soon, and if you delay coming back you will have new babes to deal with?

No, it was clear he had not thought of it and was being made to think now, and for the first time.

'And don't you care about us, Horsa? Don't you think about us?'

Here it was again, this accusation that in fact tormented Horsa. What was he supposed to be thinking? She told him: 'You know that without us there would be no new babies, you know that. But off you go – and who is going to fill our wombs? There will be no one. So there will be no new babies at all, Horsa.'

The women, listening to Maronna, were forced to take her side, even if they had only just understood it. There they stood, the women, staring at the men, every one of whom was a son, every one born out of their bodies. I often think, when scanning one of our Roman crowds, that each individual present has been born to a female, and if ever there was a common fate or destiny, then this must be it.

The women standing here, beside Maronna, were all mothers, and every male there had been dandled, fussed over, fed, cleaned, slapped, kissed, taught by a female . . . and this is such a heavy and persuasive history that I am amazed we don't remember it more often.

'Well, Horsa, what are we going to do? Have you thought of that?'

He had not. So, then, he 'did not care' – as she

said. But he did not believe he didn't care. He had not thought, that was all. So, then, if he was going off, with every adult male, then there would be no more babes, no more people, yes, she was right.

This confused him, the sheer force of it – the compulsion. A compulsion that he must think, he must accept that he was careless and irresponsible, just as she said he was. Yet these accusations of her always, and always had, made him stubborn and resisting, but he could not today tell her he wasn't listening, and that she always nagged and complained, because he was secretly thinking that she was right.

We have the scene graphically described. The women stood there in the half-dark, probably chilly in their fish-skin garments that glittered and gleamed, but were hardly good for warmth. Near them, all together, were the males, bearded, almost certainly, and wearing their familiar animal pelts. When a sea breeze lifted a layer of fur off a shoulder or a head it was hard to say if this was a pelt, or beard, or the tail of some forest beast.

It is recorded that Maronna and Horsa were 'reconciled' that night. I wonder what the original word was? How could they have become 'reconciled' when the issues that made them scream at each other remained?

We know that they all feasted, drank an alcoholic syrup invented by the men, ate forest fruit. Surely it

is hard to stay angry during a feast. Did their recon-
ciliation include sex? We know Horsa admired
Maronna, but nothing is said about Maronna's liking,
if any, for Horsa.

We Romans must assume sex took place, but is it
possible that a time will come when Rome will be
criticised for making too much of sex? I think so. But
then, this is an old man talking.

Whatever form these negotiations took, we may be
sure of one thing: the two must have been aware of
the children and the problems they made, because
both histories record it was a noisy night, the little
boys demanding attention, awake or asleep. The boys
who had been told they would go with Horsa were
overexcited and boastful, perhaps because they
were kept awake by the boys with Maronna who
were having nightmares and imagined they saw
murderous pigs everywhere. The boys who had lived
in the trees in the clearing mocked them and said
they imagined the pigs, but the fact was that two
little boys had been killed, and they were known to
all the children. Nightmares and crying out in their
sleep, tears and quarrels and tantrums . . . the girls
who wanted to be with the men, particularly as they

had only just understood that the expedition might take the men away for a good time, had to spend the night calming the children.

By the time morning came, it was a listless, weary community, and the children were – well, behaving like small children. Horsa presumably had tried to persuade Maronna of his ideas, but she persuaded him to let her see the 'fleet' that was going to set off.

She was so shocked by what she saw she assaulted Horsa, battering him with her fists and weeping that he was mad. The 'fleet', which had been assembled over months, consisted of rafts, tied together with forest rope, logs, some hollowed out, round boats made of hides stretched over enlaced circles of wood, bundles of reeds, canoes made of bark. All of these makeshift boats had been used for fishing close around the shores, and some had proved themselves safe – at least for these limited purposes. What Maronna saw we may only imagine, but what she exclaimed was, 'You want to kill them, you want to kill our children.'

Whose children? Now, that was a point indeed, relating uncomfortably to her accusation, 'Don't you care about us?' Who? The women? The small males without whom the people could have no future?

'You cannot take little children with you,' said Maronna – 'hysterical', said the men's history, 'indignant' said the women's account. What is interesting is that Horsa apparently meekly agreed.

The fact was, he had no idea small children needed so much attention – and that was because of the special conditions in the forest.

The little boys arrived after their 'escape' from the women's shore, delirious with excitement, usually with some girls, and at once went up the trees. There was also in the glade a shallow pretty stream, perfect for children. The stream was safe, and the trees too, though a watch was always kept for the big felines who prowled, and insinuated and slithered through the branches, hoping to find a small boy off guard. Had there been casualties? This is not recorded. It can be seen from this short explanation that looking after the small boys in the forest was not an arduous business. A few young men took on this task. There was only one rule to be kept. As the light drained back into the sky and the trees stood dark and hidden, every child had to be out of the trees and into the circles of firelight, later to be shut into one of the sheds for the night. Horsa scarcely had to see much of the boys, and if one broke a limb or got sick, back they went to the women.

That night under the great watching moon, when the children clamoured and demanded and made so much noise, had been a nasty revelation to Horsa.

When Maronna had seen his assembly of 'ships'

and scorned them and him, he then said he would not take the smaller boys, only older ones.

Why did he not say he would take no boys at all? I think it was pride. To capitulate completely – no, and even as it was, the men had to submit to shrieks of sarcastic laughter. We may fairly assume this laughter. Which of us males has not been subjected to it?

The smaller boys, told they were not to be with the men, rebelled and said they would run back to the forest clearing, to the trees, and wait there till the men returned.

The men had no intention of being bound by promises of return. But before they could set off, something had to be done to warn the children off the forest. All the little boys, those returning with Maronna to the women's shore, and those going with Horsa, set off, accompanied by the hunters with their weapons. It was quite a distance to the forest place on that day, when they were all tired, and there were many small boys. (*Many*: that is the word they used.) To reach the shore, and the men's place, by nightfall meant forcing the pace, and the boys who knew the trees let out cries of joy on seeing them, but then the cries and jubilation stopped. Stretched out in the middle of the forest clearing was a family of the great felines, lying as if this place were theirs. The felines were what the children had been brought here to see, and even a look at them made their backs freeze with fear. Where were the pigs who had, only a couple of days before, taken two boys? A big sow, black, with gleaming tusks and teeth, was lying across the stream and even damming it: water was spilling in shallow lakes all around her. Her size was why she and the other porkers were safe from the felines. What animal could possibly take on a herd of lean fast pigs? Perhaps a pack of dogs.

The children stood looking forlornly at their paradise, and some began to cry. It was dangerous there, despite the young hunters. Maronna set off for the women's shore, with the smaller boys – chosen arbitrarily, by height and size. The larger small boys – it sounds as if they were about ten or so – escorted by the youths, set off back to find the men. It was already afternoon. Not possible to reach the men while it was still light. This company of boys reached a shore. (How many? 'Quite a few.') They settled on a wide beach, spent the night unfed, vigilant, while unfamiliar waves crashed near them and then far away as the tide went out.

That was how the day ended when Maronna and Horsa were 'reconciled'. And the women with her resumed their usual life. It is recorded that right from the start they fretted over Horsa and the vagueness of his plans, and very much about the children he had taken with him.

The boys who were to go with Horsa were given

rules they must learn and keep. These first rules were stringent, and there were punishments. Obedience was being taught, or being attempted. If Horsa was sorry he had agreed to taking any boys at all, even older ones, he never admitted it.

The first day showed that Horsa had had no idea of what he was taking on.

Imagine the excitement of the boys, each with his raft or a bundle of reeds, or even a tree trunk, setting off with the men on the first stage of the journey. They were wild, paddling with sticks or several bound together, or even their hands, getting in the way of the men in their larger vessels. They kept falling in and had to be rescued. They could all swim, of course, no question of their drowning, these water babies, but the 'fleet' planned by Horsa and his aides had to go slowly, the little boys took up so much of their attention. By the end of the first day it was clear: if the expedition was to make any progress the little boys would have to be removed from it. Horsa issued an edict. No boy could be part of the 'fleet', join the men, if he had not achieved his man's body. Did that mean puberty? Did it mean older? What it certainly did mean was a crowd of boys sulking, angry, weeping, saying it wasn't fair.

But Horsa was adamant. The smaller boys would be on the shore, and they would be watched over by the youths, the hunters and trackers, and this part of

Horsa's company would go along the shore parallel to the men in their boats. In the evenings they would all meet up by the fires and for the feasting. . . . Yes, there was too much of the theoretical here even for Horsa who is revealed by this 'edict' to be one of those leaders who would expect difficulties simply to melt away.

A shore has inlets, the mouths of rivers, some large; marshes, cliffs, and although watched over by the big boys, these children were bound to have a hard time working along that shore. And there were wild animals, too. All the boys had weapons. What weapons? Mentioned are knives, both seashell splinters and of sharpened bone, a kind of catapult, deadly even for big animals, bows and arrows. These little boys knew how to defend themselves. But they were soon tired out and complaining, and behaved, in short, like children, crying and subject to tantrums and tempers. The older boys complained. So the order was softened. Keeping parallel with the fleet of little ships meant running along the beaches, not going further inland, so the whole expedition had sometimes to wait for days while the children negotiated some mangrove swamp or big cliff. More than once the 'fleet' had to come in and lift the little boys round an obstacle, and when this happened they clamoured to be allowed to join the main party on their improvised boats. Complaints and tears and trouble, and there are songs from that time, sardonic songs, telling of the brave warriors who had often to leave their adventures and look after children.

How Horsa must have cursed his decision ever to allow children, yet he did not voice what he felt.

Before the expedition had gone too far away, some girls returned to the women's shore, and always took some boys with them. This was for their own safety, because of wild animals, but it may be assumed that Horsa was glad to get rid of a boy or two or more when he could. Meanwhile the women's shore became ever more crowded and noisy and inconvenient.

The returning girls said that journeying with Horsa was difficult, not least because there were not enough girls to match the men. There is mention – for the very first time in our histories – that there were couples, recognised pairs. Horsa did not like this; it caused dissension, even to the point of fighting and quarrelling over the girls.

Horsa was too much of a tyrant, said the returning girls.

Horsa . . . who, in fact, was he? First, he – or a Horsa – had ended the fighting among the different groups in the forest, taking command, making a whole from many subdivisions. 'The forest became safe,' say the women's histories, 'and we could go anywhere there, unharmed, provided we went in groups.'

That was surely Horsa's best self, the brilliant

commander whom everyone was happy to obey. And then he organised the forest life, keeping the little boys safe in their trees, choosing the hunters and trackers, and who would look after the clearing, the sheds and the lean-tos and the fires. The predators who prowled and watched the company were kept at a distance. Yet he was also the leader who brought the expedition to disaster. Two different people? Names, in those old days, were attached to qualities: Maronna seemed always to be the name of the women's leader. Horsa had diplomacy and tact, necessary for a commander of many men (how many?), but he did not know how to manage his expedition, which the women called foolhardy, dangerous, ill-planned, stupid. And Horsa's adventure turned out to be all those things.

For a long time, at least the period of a pregnancy, the seas the 'fleet' travelled over were serene, warm and gentle. The dug-outs and logs, the bundles of reeds and coracles, went happily along by the beaches, well in sight of the little boys, and it was easy to come in to the warm sands for meals, or for the night. Nothing was difficult, then, at the beginning.

Then there was something Horsa could not have avoided, and he must have reckoned with the possibility: there was a big storm, and all the little craft, which so comfortably and pleasurably carried those young men along, were smashed and lay wrecked along the beaches, together with other refuse from the storm. To reassemble the little craft was not a big challenge, and a few little vessels were put together, but Horsa did not at once suggest setting forth. They all camped along the beaches, made their great fires, hunted in the forests, cooked their meat, sent parties inland for fruit and green stuff – and seemed to be waiting. For what? The fact was the expedition had failed, and the smashed craft were only a confirmation of that.

The trouble was the little boys – who, we must remember, cannot be compared with our children of the same age. They were ten, eleven, twelve, did not 'have their man's bodies' yet, but could use all the weapons, could hunt with the hunters and track with the trackers, but they were rebellious and complaining, and dissatisfied with everything. Day after day, arduously clambering along these shores, which were sometimes easy but often not, watching for the arrival of the men from the sea, this was not what their early excitement for 'adventure' had promised. And they were tired, too. Some were children as young as seven or eight, if they had been well grown for their ages at the time Maronna had set off home, taking the younger ones. They sometimes wanted their mothers, or at least the women who liked children enough to be given childcaring as their work by Maronna. Horsa had known almost from the start that bringing the boys had been a mistake, but they were a long way from home – if home was the forest – and a longer way from the women's shore.

He planned to send all the boys back home, with the young men as guards, but when the plan was put to them the youths said no, to have to look after these peevish disobedient children for long and difficult travelling – no. We do not have another record of his young men saying no to Horsa. Then that meant the whole expedition would have simply to confess failure and go home?

That would not be easy, would it? To say to the ever scornful Maronna that she was right – bad enough. But there was worse. Horsa had said he wanted to find out if, by following the shore, he would one day simply return to where they had started out – suddenly see the women on their rocks and know they had made a full circle of their land. And more, Horsa wanted to find another land, other shores, other – people? That was never ever suggested. But surely these people must sometimes have wondered if somewhere others like themselves lived as they did, wondering if they were alone in the seas and the forests?

To go home to Maronna and the women and say . . . I find it hard to imagine words Horsa would use.

But if the young men's need from the time they were little boys had been to distance themselves from the women, they did now miss the ease of the visiting, women to men, men to women. And did they miss, too, the scolding and the advice?

'Stupid, stupid, stupid – did you really think you could make little children into adults simply by treating them like adults? Did you really imagine that little boys would behave like your obedient young hunters because it would suit you if they did?'

Horsa took some of his men walking along the beaches, to see what he might find; he took them on trips inland to high points, like very tall trees or hills, any lookout where they might spy something that would justify Horsa's hopes.

Time passed. And now at last a happening which dated events, for them as well as for us.

There were several pregnant girls and their size and condition caused Horsa many difficulties.

They gave birth and then the long balmy beaches where they camped and feasted, male beaches, full of mostly men, heard the wails of infants. Horsa was appalled, and so were all the young men. This is what they had run away from – wasn't it?

'Well, what did you expect? Girls give birth and babies cry, and you have to feed the babes and wash them and keep them warm – had you not thought of that? Idiots, fools, oh you make us lose patience with you . . . Horsa, do you mean to say you didn't know this was going to happen? Don't you remember we told you if you took girls with you they would get pregnant?'

Imagined scoldings and the words, '. . . and so what
are you going to do now?'

A babe died. A certain fly inhabited this beach,
yellowish flies settling in swarms anywhere they could
find food, like detritus washed in from the sea, rotting
fish or dead sea animals, seabirds, seaweed and, as
soon as the light went, the almost naked bodies of
the boys and men who remembered that their aprons
of feathers and leaves did have their uses.

The fires were built tall and hot, and they all
crowded in as close as they dared to the flames. The
babe that died was swollen with bites and the girls
tried to keep their infants safe by bathing them contin-
uously in the waves – which made their skins pucker
and become inflamed.

Horsa ordered an exodus, but it was only to move
along to a beach where the flies were not. One sandy
beach is like another for its amenities.

But the infants cried and were fretful, and the girls
complained. They had come on this trip because they
liked mating and the comradeship of men, but now
they had gone off sex, and would not give ease to
the men and the boys.

So what use were they? the boys grumbled. 'What
use?' argued the girls. 'Aren't we making a new generation of people?'

But they are a horrid nuisance, said the boys.

They had come such a long way, measured by time,

at least nine months, though there had been stops and slows on the road. Measured by distance – but they did not know how to do that.

How long would it take them to return? Return where? The glade in the forest? Their trees, which they dreamed of – what a wondrous time that had been, the safety of the great trees. Many of the young men and boys were saying they had been mad ever to leave. All that was needed were well-armed guards around the edges of the glade, to keep off the marauding pigs and the creeping felines.

But for some reason no one wanted to do this: journeys are to get somewhere, find something, to discover, take possession . . . grumbling was not helping them. So what was to be done?

Another babe died, and the sounds of weeping women were added to the babies' crying. These boys could not remember babes dying from sickness. Presumably it *was* sickness that was taking these infants off?

The girls who had lost infants became listless, and wept or lay about, their arms over their faces, silent, suffering . . . and milk dripped from their breasts. Oh, horrible, unseemly, and the boys showed their dislike, and yet these were girls who had shared their adventures and were comrades, like the boys – but then they spoiled everything by getting pregnant and then all the rest of the unpleasant sights and sounds. As for the very little boys, they were revolted.

How much nicer it had been in the forest, not too far from the women's shore. Girls could visit, got what they had come for – to have their wombs enlivened – and then they went back home again and there were new girls, and they were helpful and useful, so handy about the glade, and particularly so good with broken limbs and little sicknesses. And look at them now, preoccupied with their noisy infants, or lying silent and unhappy. And they would not be kind to the boys.

And now there was a big halt in the histories. Horsa's expedition and the destruction of The Cleft marked an end. It was a beginning too, of the villages in the forests. But then they did not know there would be villages. The chroniclers did not know it. The words 'Horsa did not know where he was' ended one long section of the histories.

'It takes one to know one!' I can tell when an historian is looking back to a time far from his or her own and is uncomfortable because times have changed.

What did it mean to the new chroniclers to say: 'Horsa did not know where he was.' Where were they, these new voices? In the villages in the forests. We do not know how many villages there were, nor how many people lived in them. What the chroniclers felt they must emphasise was that every village had a double palisade round it, to keep out the animals. They knew where they were. For one thing, they were not far from the women's settlements along the shores. It took time for the women – ages? – to consent to leave the sea and move in with the men, and only then if they were within walking distance of the shore. So when the village chroniclers said, 'Horsa did not know where he was,' we must assume they knew where they were. The exploits of Horsa and his mad trip across the waves had by then become recognised in songs and tales for telling around the fires.

I do not think that we Romans may easily imagine what it meant – Horsa not knowing where he was. We Romans are taught 'where we are' in a thousand ways. When our legions return from Gaul, from the lands of the Germans, from Dacia, they tell us where they have been. When invaders threaten Rome we know where they are from. Our ships travel the seas, go north even to Britain, to Egypt, and our slaves know lands we hardly have heard of. We Romans know where we are, and even a young child is taught to say, 'This Rome of ours does not contain all that is known.' And this child would know that if he stood on a beach and saw ahead a curving further shore, it might very well be the other side of a bay, and to get there would only need some days' travelling from where he stands to reach that shore.

But think of Horsa, and what he knew. He knew the rocky and choppy waves of the women's shore. He knew the great river and the forests of the eagles' valley. He knew the forest glade and its great trees and the ways from it to the women. So when Horsa stood on his beach – but he did not know where this beach was – looking ahead across the waves, he had no idea that he might be in a bay and he was staring at another part of it. Oh yes, he knew bays from his fleet's progress around the shores from their starting place where he had said goodbye to Maronna. Little bays, little promontories. Did he have words for them? The later historians in the villages knew what a bay was, a promontory, because Horsa's mad dash across the waves had taught them: this was no bay, small or large, where Horsa and his men idled on his beach, not knowing what to do. I repeat, 'Horsa did not know where he was' represents a limitation of knowledge that no Roman may easily imagine.

Horsa did not idle there alone. His older young men were with him, when not hunting in the forests. We know this was no contented group of men.

'Horsa was much troubled by the women and their small children and the little boys, whom he could not control.'

The little boys thought of themselves as big boys, and emulated the hunters and the food gatherers. How many were they? Taking into account that some had left with the women who had gone home, our guess (this can only be a guess) is that they were perhaps twenty, not many more. 'Some' is the helpful word used by the chroniclers. They were very pleased with their accomplishments, would come swaggering back to the beach with the animals they had killed, just like the youths who had achieved their men's bodies. They were tough and fearless, and did not obey Horsa, obeyed nobody. They might go off in a band by themselves for a day or two. More than once one was killed by a boar or a pack of dogs. Horsa didn't know what to do with them. Attempts were made to attach a few to the hunting bands of the big youths, to include them into the general whole, but these little boys – who were very unlike any little boy we know – were proud of their independence. They even elected a leader, a boy not older than they were, but stronger and the most brave. They might apply to the girls, those who were ready to be friendly, for help with a broken limb, or a wound. It is recorded the girls were afraid of these wild boys who were a long way from being described as 'little'. Little boys they were not. And the big youths, hunting, encountering a band of these boys, were wary with them, as if they were enemies. There were some fights between the grown youths and 'little boys' who, if they were half the size of the grown men, were just as strong and wily and skilled in the ways of the forest.

What was Horsa going to do with these boys, who when asked if they would go back to the women, laughed or shouted, 'No, no, never.'

Horsa's friend, who accompanied him on his venture, was with him on their comfortable beach, and they endlessly argued about what they would do. It is clear they weren't in any hurry to do anything.

They had wanted to find out if this land of theirs was an island but the concept 'island' was not what we Romans would accept as island. They had thought thus: they might suddenly one morning see that they had sailed so far they would see the women's shore just ahead of them, with the cliffs and caves of The Cleft. So in their minds was the idea of a circumference, an end where a beginning had been. 'Island' was used by the later village chroniclers. The journey of the 'fleet' going just outside where the sea broke on the beaches had seemed endless. If they did know where they had set off, then they had no idea where this 'end' was. How did they know this journeying was not endless? How did they know this land of theirs was not so large they might encompass it? In their elation at setting out these thoughts had not come near them.

Horsa and his companions, the young men, the hunters and trackers when not on a trip into the trees, idled about the bonfires at night, tried to reason with the 'little boys', listened to the seas washing in and out with their endless messages of movement, impermanence, and stared out at a horizon . . . and perhaps it was at that moment, for the very first time ever,

that the idea of a bay, a very large bay, became something in their minds they might refer to. Did they
find a word for 'bay' and use it? They could at least
make a short trip and see what they could find. To
make boats of bundles of reeds, of little platforms
and branches, was not difficult. A few – very few,
probably two or three – of the big men, with Horsa
as leader, went secretly on to a little flotilla of these
'boats', leaving at a time when the 'little boys' were
not around, and they went on along the coast. I
imagine – it is hard not to think like this – that Horsa
might have thought of going off altogether, and abandoning the little boys. But that meant the girls and
their infants too, and the pregnant ones as well. In
Horsa's mind rang Maronna's words, 'Don't you care
about us, Horsa?' And that meant more now to him
than it had then. Horsa knew, if perhaps not all of
this company did, that to produce infants men were
needed. 'Don't you care about us?' Horsa must have
thought that the women were months of travelling
away (this would have been thought of, probably, as
time passing, not space covered) and that they must
be getting frantic, waiting for the men. It is known
they all knew, men and women, that an interval
elapsed between mating and the birth, though with
these people who apparently could not master
numbers in any combination or means of reckoning,
the 'interval' would have been vague. But time had

passed, and Horsa heard much too often, 'Don't you care about us?'

Did Horsa care about what we call a continuation of our race in the same way as we do? For instance, for pregnant slaves we pay higher prices than for older women or ones with flat bellies.

In the forest glade, did he now take trouble over guarding and caring for the little boys? And we come back to this question we cannot answer: did he think about the people? When Maronna said, 'Don't you care about us?' did she mean all of them, males and females, Clefts and the once-upon-a-time Monsters? Who was 'us'?

Meanwhile Horsa went on for one day, two, three, stopping for the night when the waves were rough, and the shore unwound in front of him with no end. And looking back over their shoulders, they could see a streak or line of colour where they had stared for a long time now, and wondered if that was simply a curving continuation of the shore they stood on.

They turned back: they could not simply go on, abandoning the others.

Again in their place, where the girls and their infants greeted them in a way that said their thoughts had been that they had been abandoned, the young men stared out in front of them, and saw, without really seeing, at the very edge where sea and sky met, a line of distant colour that did not change its place. Like a shore. Some said it was a shore – it had to be – none of them could easily conceive of a bay so large that its opposite sides were almost out of sight. It was not easy to accept that what they were looking at was a place they could travel to. Or could have done, if they had large enough boats. What would they find? A country where a boy, with or without his man's body, would not be treated as an infant? Young women whose bellies did not swell up and then give birth to howling infants? Friendly girls who never grew sad and sulky and refused to play?

Horsa, who was in a fever because of this shore tinted like a dream, said that until the storm they had all done very well in their fragments of boats: they had skulled and rowed and paddled for weeks, for months – for ages – then; and the waves had been kind to them, and the journey now seemed like a wonderful thing. Yes, insisted Horsa: they could easily make a craft fit enough to take them across to that shore that seemed to beckon him, and they would head out over easy pretty waves and find . . .

A raft of bundles of reeds was fitted together, bigger and stronger than any raft they had made before. The big boys and the little clamoured to be taken on this adventure, but were promised another trip, if this one was successful. Horsa and his friend, whose name we have never known, set out at dawn towards a streak that in this light was pinky-pearl, with a line of dark-blue cloud over it.

They had expected to reach there soon – that was the word used by the chroniclers. Not 'by evening' or 'after a short time', but soon. They were taking much longer than they expected. They laboured with their paddles, and went on, and on, but that beckoning shore did not come any closer. It was long past midday, and on they went, and when it was already getting dusk they were within a distance of a new land, if it was that – but they had no idea what it could be. Beaches again, and trees of a kind they had not seen. It was the trees that seduced them into thinking this place was altogether better, richer, more beautiful than their own. The trees as described by people who had never seen anything like them sound like palms, and there were great white birds in them, with trailing feathers like the fronds of the palms. Everything they looked at seemed remarkable and new, and all they wanted was to land their flimsy craft, which was ready to fall apart after so long over the waves much taller than they had become used to, and then a new life would begin, and . . .

It was late afternoon and the light was dimming and stars filling the sky, and Horsa looked up at his constellation and thought that it looked down on him. It was essential they must land, soon, soon, but then their fragile support began to rock and toss on

the waves, and a wind came straight towards them
from this gleaming promise of a shore, a wind that
reminded them of the storm that wrecked their boats.
The dark cloud that settled over the land blew towards
them in thin black streams, and they found they were
being blown back to where they had come from.
Blown fast and then faster, they were being skimmed
over now tall and choppy waves while they clung to
a handful of reeds that was all that was left of the
raft, which fell apart and dissolved into the sea. Horsa
and his friend were being tossed like foam on the
waves, and then spun and tumbled, and the two were
flung on to the beach they had left at dawn, violently,
cruelly. Night had come long ago, the fires were
flaring all along the beaches. The young man who
was Horsa's friend was lying still, bent and broken,
and he did not respond and never came to life. Horsa's
leg was smashed, it was twisted and he lay on the
warm sand and sobbed from pain but even more from
disappointment.

And now I really cannot stop myself from inter-
vening again. It is because I feel so much for that
youngster there, Horsa, lying hurt on the sand and
dreaming of that other place, which he could not reach.
He did try, though . . . I feel that he is my younger self,
perhaps even a son. What was he longing for, when

he saw that distant shore and wanted it? I know there are those who think the Greeks said the last word on aspirations. But I am not one to yield to the Greeks, not in this field. I am of the party that believes we Romans have bettered the Greeks. Horsa was not after finer dimensions in life, I see him as an ancestor of us, the Romans. What we see we need to conquer; what we know is there we have to know too. Horsa was in himself a coloniser, but that was before the word and idea was born. I see poor Horsa lying there crippled and think of how Rome has hurt itself in our need to expand, to have. I think of my two poor sons, lying somewhere in those northern forests. Rome has to outleap itself, has to grow, has to reach out. Far and further, wide and wider, our Roman empire's bounds are set. Why should there ever be an end to us, to Rome, to our boundaries? Subject peoples may fight us, but they never can stop us. I sometimes imagine how all the known world will be Roman, subject to our beneficent rule, to Roman peace, Roman laws and justice, Roman efficiency. Truly we make deserts bloom and the lands we conquer blossom. Some greater power than human guides us, leads us, points where our legions must go next. And if there are those who crit- icise us, then I have only one reply. Why, then, if we lack the qualities needed to make the whole earth flourish, why does everyone want to be a Roman citizen? All, everybody, from any part of our empire and beyond, wants to be a free man inside Roman law, Roman peace. Answer that, then, you carpers and doubters. As for me, I imagine poor Horsa, lying there on his patch of sand, crippled because of his need to know that other wonderful land – and I think of him, secretly, as a Roman. One of us. Ours.

He lay like a child with his arm across his face, and when he could speak and the others wanted to listen, he told about the wonders of the other shore. For while this land, their own, had noble trees and birds and animals, whose eyes gleamed at them from the bushes, the shore he had failed to reach and from which he had been ejected so fiercely by the tyrant wind, this land, the new one, was seductive and desirable in a way their own land could never be.

But the others did not seem inclined to listen. There were tasks, and difficulties, first of all the disposal of the dead youth's body, thrown into the waves, which brought it back again to lie brokenly not far from Horsa. One of the girls who had lost a baby came to insist that the sea did not accept the dead; it was much better to bury this body. So Horsa's comrade was put under the sand and Horsa lay nearby and thought that it could have been himself who disappeared into the choking sand. Another girl brought him water and food at the evening's feast, but what all these big boys and young men were talking about was the smaller boys, who had brought back a carcass from their hunting, but were cooking it at a separate bonfire not far away, instead of adding it, as was usually done, to the common supply. The children were dancing and singing, wild with their independence and mocking their elders who were around their own fires. Horsa shouted at them to come over and join the main feast but the children ignored him. Horsa was being generally ignored, and he did not understand it, nor did he see that an air of hilarity and anarchy that prevailed was because he was not there, leader of them all, in command, always visible as central focus of authority. No, he was lying on the sand, or crawling, trying to sit up, and weak with pain.

The sea had tossed up a piece of wood, and Horsa grabbed it, tried to raise himself up on it. People turned to stare and then to smile, glancing at each other; the crooked stick beside the crooked leg was like a mocking echo and the little boys at the other fire, seeing Horsa with three legs, one dangling, began to jeer and point. The older youths did the same. Horsa stood tottering, holding hard on to the stick, but then he fell and there was a shout of laughter. Horsa tried to rise, but failed. The girl who had lost her baby came to lift him, but she failed. She wandered off. Horsa lay, helpless and like a shamed beast. He felt he had become cast out from them, and when the little boys came over to stand around him, pointing and jeering, he lay huddled into the sand, trying to be invisible. They wandered off too, back into the forests near the shore. The big boys were planning a hunt for tomorrow. No one seemed to see him. He had to crawl away from them all to meet a demand of his bowels, and when he returned lay behind a long rock that hid most of him. No one spoke to him. He did not understand what he felt. He had always been whole and strong and handsome, and he wished he could disappear altogether.

In the morning he woke, in bad pain, raging with thirst – and had to crawl slowly to the container where the water was. He could not lift the great seashell. Few of the others were awake. The older youths had gone off to hunt, the little boys were not there. Some girls with their babes, apart from the main body of people, saw him and did not seem to want to help him. At last, seeing that he was going to let slip the shell and waste the water, a girl did come and give him water. She was not unkind, but he was used to a greater . . . what was it he lacked, and what was it she did not offer him? It was respect, which he always had, and needed.

Then, sated with water, he turned to look at the sea and there, far away, where the sea and sky met, was the gleam of light which he knew was his imagined place, his land where he would find everything he wanted – though until he had seen the pinky-pearl shores where the great white birds decorated the trees like dreams, he had no idea what he longed for. He was there sheltering from the fierce sun in the shadow of the rocks, staring, always staring, while the enticing shore changed colour as the sun moved. No one came to offer him help, water, food, or to talk to him. He wanted so much to tell them all about this wondrous place he had seen, which he had nearly reached, where . . .

If you have had authority all your life, because of your nature, something you never knew you had, and then you lose it, then it is hard even to ask the right questions. What was it he had lost? What now did he lack that all the others had needed in him? Horsa had not decided to be a leader, the uniter of the many warring groups – if it was he who had personally done this thing, and not someone from whom he had inherited authority – he had not fought for authority over others, but had never not known it. Why now did his comrades seem to be deaf when he spoke to them? The same girl, whom he called to bring him water and did answer, sat near him while he talked about his wondrous land that he had seen, actually seen with his own eyes, before the wind blasted him back across the waves to his own beach. Then she said that he must not lie there mumbling about his vision, the others were saying he had gone mad, and they were all disturbed by him. This enterprise of theirs was failing, and in dangerous ways. Decisions should be made and who was to make them? She seemed to take it for granted it could not be crippled and crawling Horsa. He, Horsa, must choose one of the older youths to work with him and make some kind of central command. While Horsa was muttering in his delirium about this other land, dangerous things happened.

The young men were taking no notice of Horsa, who was trying to stagger around on his crooked stick. The girls were no better. They had fewer infants, for some had died, and there were no girls swelling up with pregnancy. They kept apart from the men, when they could, in a group, though they got their share of food. The little boys sometimes joined in the general evening feasts, but mostly they were off some-where: their voices could at times be heard echoing from the forest. There was no question now of controlling them. Children they might be, but if they had not achieved their men's bodies they were as brave and skilled as the men who, the truth was, were afraid to tackle them.

Some kind of central command or authority, it seemed, the girls were demanding and when they tried to assume control of the young boys, they were told they were just Clefts, and must shut up.

Another babe had been born and the young men told the girls to keep to themselves with their noisy infants, and so the girls were always at a little distance from the general community.

Horsa could not get any of the big boys to take him on, or even accept him as a comrade. No one wanted to listen to his talk of the other land, which at sunset gleamed in its inky-pearl and gold colours under the heavy blue cloud.

No one wanted Horsa at all.

And yet, with the crippling of Horsa some kind of unifying spirit had finally gone from the company. How could it be possible, he wondered, lying wounded in the shade of his rock, that recently he had stood among these people as a being stronger, better, than they, and everything he said was attended to?

Except, of course, for the little boys: it had been some time now since they had listened to anyone.

Maeve, the girl who could be kindly and who had warned Horsa, came to tell him that the little boys had found a cave, or a system of caves, where they spent their time. Had he not noticed that they had not been around with the others recently? This was a shock to Horsa. He had not noticed. He seemed to notice nothing but his pain, his heavy dragging limb. He forced himself upright, using the stick, and practised walking, or rather pulling himself about, over the sand.

Once he was on his feet, even though he could not let go of the supporting stick, it seemed people saw him again. They did not want to listen to his tales of the new land, but when he spoke they did pay attention.

Maeve asked about the children, and the young men were uncomfortable and even impatient. What were they supposed to do? Horsa saw that the absence of the children troubled the older boys and that there had been discussions and decisions among them he had not noticed.

Standing, Horsa said he must be taken up to this cave, or caves, and some kind of authority seemed to have returned to him, because with the aid of his stick, and a youth on either side, supporting him he dragged himself up the side of a cliff behind their beach and saw the entrance to a cavern that had a path to it, telling them all that the little boys used it well – and often.

And now here is a hint as to how many the children were. To make a 'well-used' path takes more than, let's say, four, or six, or even ten; or perhaps we are seeing here a measure of time. These people had been on this new shore of theirs for much longer than they supposed. And outside the cavern's mouth was a space made by the hacking away of bushes and grass. From there the boys could look down at the beach where their elders built their fires and at meals where they should have been too, with their contributions from the hunt. Very easy was it to imagine the childish sniggers and jeers of the children who were so well out of reach of supervision.

The cave itself was high, and large; on either side it fell into dark edges where it was easy to understand that no one, child or adult, would want to go. The main cave was smooth, and had been used – perhaps was used now – by animals. On some low rocks were the little boys' possessions: some animal skins, some fish-skin loincloths, a large shell with water, and some meat from a past supper. The smell was not pleasant. And where were the children? Not a sign of them. The adults called, shouted, even threatened and commanded, but silence answered them. Either the children had gone hunting, or they had taken themselves far into the cave, and were waiting to be left alone again. Horsa suggested to the big boys that they might go a little way into the back of the cave and saw them agreeing, but with reluctance: the big tunnel at the cave's back almost at once bifurcated. It seemed some of the youths had already gone a little way into the rear of the cave and had found a maze of caves. Horsa could see the young men were embarrassed, even ashamed. Yes, they should have kept an eye on the little boys, if they could be called that, while Horsa had been weak and not himself.

Horsa suggested some might climb up here at evening, to see if the children had returned; yes, but one called out that he wouldn't want to go far into this cave or any of them: there were animals, you could hear them. Then another said that he had to say he would not like to encounter the children in the dark, if he was by himself. Horsa stood, holding himself on his stick, trembling with weakness still, and listened to their talk. There were systems of caves, and tunnels between them, and deep underground rivers, and even lakes. If any attempt was to be made on the lines of recovering the children then it would have to be in the day, and at least two search parties, with the strongest ropes they could make out of the forest, and torches. If one group got lost, then another could go and rescue them. Horsa said, 'We can't just leave the children, if they are lost somewhere.' Then, knowing it sounded less than convincing, he said, 'After all, we forget, they are only children' – and saw the eyes of his companions turn towards him, speculatively, surprised, some disbelieving. 'Children' he was calling those dangerous boys?

Horsa stood waiting till the youths were well out of the cave before grasping his stick and staggering after them. And now Maeve came to aid him. Outside, on the platform where were the scuffed remains of evening fires, Horsa grasped tight to a young tree trunk, and closed his eyes to recover. When he opened them, Maeve was still holding him up and he was staring straight out to sea where a line of shining light, with dark cloud above, told him that he was looking at his other land. From up here, high on the cliff, it stretched a good way along the horizon. And was it deep, as well? Horsa strained and could not see. How far away was it? Did he ever ask himself, or did he measure its distance by the slow voyage he and his friend had made towards it, then the rapid skimming of them both back over the waves? He could have leaped into the hot summer's day air and taken two steps towards *his* place, which waited for him. Maeve, seeing how he stared, looked too, but said, 'Horsa, the others don't like it, when you stare over there. What is it that you see? There are always clouds building up there, we can all see that.' It seemed then to Horsa that light flashed up from the 'cloud'. Lightning? What could be making that flash, which was like a signal to him: 'I am here, don't forget.'

Pressured gently by Maeve's strong arm, Horsa got down the hill to the beach. He did stumble, but picked himself up and hoped the others hadn't seen him fall. Maeve patiently held him till he reached the level of the beach and he sat on a rock and waited till his weakness left him.

And now when they lit their supper fires on the beach, they looked up the cliff path to catch sight of the children, if they were there. They looked up to see if there was a fire burning outside the cave. Night

226

after night they waited, and a heaviness settled on them all. There were mutters that the children were lost. Then, as had been suggested, parties with ropes and torches set off at midday when the light was strongest and might penetrate a little way into the caves, and came up to report that there were labyrinths, dangerous ones, and it was easy to imagine children being swept away by the rivers, or falling down precipices. They called, they shouted, in cave after cave, and though that was hard, in that echoing system of caves and caverns where any voice was multiplied, they believed they did hear the cries of lost children, who were calling for help, though probably what was being heard were the voices of seabirds on the cliffs, or even animals who lived in the caves. There was another attempt to penetrate deeper, but the trouble was there was not just one cave, or system, but many, and now they had to believe the children were indeed lost. Horsa said they must wait, just in case the boys turned up, but the talk was for them all to move on and away from this beach, which it was felt was unlucky.

'Don't you care about us, Horsa?' And Horsa heard Maronna's voice in his dreams and in the sound of the waves and in the wind. 'Don't you care, Horsa?'

And then some boys were found in the labyrinth, 'some'. And they were like skeletons. So that is a clue. Healthy little boys don't become all bones in a

day or so. They were frightened and their eyes 'stared'.
Something very bad had frightened them. They were
in a hole deep down a shaft. The big boys had nearly
not gone further, but taunts from their fellows of
'Cowards! You are scared' made them go further than
they should have gone. If the underground waters
had shifted, as they do, real skeletons would have
been found. The boys at first could not eat, then ate
a great deal, and no one could move until they were
fit to travel. They refused to go down into the caves
again. In the way of children they swore they would
rather die than ever go into any cave. What had
happened to the other children they did not know,
or were too afraid to say. Their interlocutors heard
names: 'Brian' fell into a river; 'Big Bear' fell into a
shaft; 'Runner' was caught by a big snake. So at least
they had these names to take back to the waiting
women – who were more and more on their minds.

For a long time no one had thought of or mentioned
the women but now, and because of the lost children,
they talked of Maronna and what she would say if
she knew. The men were more and more saying how
it was long past the time for going back. This means
that they did know not only that it was they who
put babes into wombs, but that time was important
– periods of time. These, our ancestors, our so distant
forebears, never spoke, as far as we can tell from
their records, of how they measured time, but did at

least match the getting of babies with time. The men around their great fires, which sent long scarlet and gold reflections across the waves when they were near and not out on a tide, spoke of the women and their waiting and, apart from the jokes which I am sure we may deduce were made (I imagine a group of legionnaires around their fires, thinking of waiting women), said that Maronna would be anxious, she would be angry with them when they did turn up. And when did they expect that would be?

The plan was to go on around the island as far as they could, or until they came on the women's shore. Did they know by then it might be an island? *We* know, and that gives a shape and a limit to our imaginings of their journey. There were islands in the great river in the valley, and in their slow measuring of the shores in their argosy they must have encountered islands, that is, land by itself where waves washed around it. Did Horsa see his tempting captivating shore as the edge of an island? He never used the word. Perhaps the idea of his shining place as something with a circumference would have put a shadow on his thought of it.

While the little boys were recuperating – and the histories make it clear this was as much a mental recovery as physical, something else happened. The big boys with a leaning towards a sympathetic understanding of badly shocked children spent time with them, talking and listening, and so did the girls, but then one girl gave birth and at once the babe died. This shocked them all. Why should this new baby die, without any reason, and without much warning? There were no flies on this beach, with their poisonous stings. And for the first time we read that this baby was valued, when so many had disappeared. The bereft mother was distraught, and while they found her wailings and mourning irritating, they were not as impatient with her as they had been with earlier weeping mothers. Again there was talk of Maronna: why were babies dying here, with them, when as far as they could remember, they didn't with the women?

The party setting off to 'go home' – and this phrase was actually used, showing how sentiments had changed – was not as carefree as it had been. When the children were judged well enough to travel, and the newly bereft girl too, they had to debate about where to set off.

The young hunters, chasing a hare through undergrowth, had found what they believed to be a main cave, high and wide, whose depths did not fragment into a hundred small tunnels, but ran back straight and level away from the cliff. It was, it seemed, a roadway for animals. Large and small animals lived there, or had until the noise and disturbance of the hunters sent them away. The prints were everywhere in the dust of the cave. And here we are again: what animals? Giant bears? Pigs? Great cats? How very strange these minds are to us, that knew no need to ask, what? How many? How?

The animals had fled but apparently the youths did not seem to connect their disappearance with the din they made, the running feet, the shouts, the yells, the stones flung at cave walls to reverberate. Before deciding on the main cave as at least the start of their return, some girls went into the very first cave and called the names of the lost boys, and then as far in as they dared. And here is a hint that they might have been missing brothers, or even sons. They called names and listened, called and listened, but heard only their own voices reiterating the echoes of names.

It was said around the fires that it was as well Maronna had insisted on taking some of the little boys back with her. 'Otherwise we would have no boys to grow up and become like us.' And this was repeated sagely by all the youths, once it was said by someone. 'Just think! Suppose there were no children born – what then?'

Horsa said to them that even as things were there would be a time when the generation of youths who hunted and defended them all would be few. 'It will be a dangerous time, while we wait for the boys we have to grow up.'

And this thought made even greater care and attention go into their watch over the boys they had left, who were being difficult and nervous after their ordeal. They still said they could not go down into this new cave, which was not nearly as hazardous as earlier caves. It was not completely dark, and had many exits up to the forests above where Horsa travelled. There were shafts of sunlight into this cave, and the aromas of trees and fresh water stronger even than the smell of animals. Below the great cave were systems of tunnels and holes, and no one ventured down there. But it did become a game to see how far they could go along the cavern before they found obstacles. There were sometimes mounds of debris from a fall in the roof, or a shaft down, so big they had to walk carefully round it. They were going easily along, without much danger; and this was made pleasanter because it was so easy to call up to Horsa, travelling above with the small boys. His hurt leg made it hard for him to go as fast as the boys, who were recovering well, but the party on the forest floor and the one below, in the cave, stopped often at the same time, to have a meal together, and to check that everyone was still there.

By now it had become clear to them all that this land was as riddled as an old piece of wood that the borers had got at. Caves and tunnels and wells and great worlds of underground rivers and lakes. Who would ever have suspected this if the little boys had not made a home for themselves high on the cliff above the beach?

It is not comfortable for me to think of the tunnels and caves undermining the surface of the island – a maze, a labyrinth, like a hidden truth to our known world. When I was young I never thought of the catacombs. Why should I? For me death and the deathly were postponed for many years. But now I, and all Romans, have to remember the catacombs. Criminals and escaped slaves and prisoners hide there, and now, too, the Christians, wicked impious fanatics who it is said by some set fire to our Rome. Only because the wind veered in time was my house spared by the flames. Fire, crime, mockery of our laws and our gods are always with me.

There were soon not two, but more parties. While the great cavern that ran on for ever, so it seemed, provided a wealth of thrills and excitements every day, they were bound to get tired of it, and some youths came up to travel with Horsa and the little boys till that pace was too slow and they went off and found beaches, which they had to assume were different from their former beach. The sun went down into the sea in a way that reminded them of the women's shore. Did that tell them anything? Did they know they were now going straight towards the women? If *straight* is a word to use, with many parties exploring here and there, going off and coming back. The one place no one wanted to visit now were the beaches, which were not far away on their right sides – if they had decided yet, our ancestors, that there was a left and a right, and that this was a measurement they could use. But the beaches had lost their attraction. They had been on beaches, and by them, for so long now. There was nothing they did not know about beaches and the seas that changed even as you looked at them.

Horsa, being told by one of the girls that from a little hill you could see right across the tops of trees to a stretch of sea where *his* shores gleamed, climbed up. They seemed so close, the pink-pearl streaks like the inside of a shell, that seemed always to carry a marker of a dark-blue cloud. He sat up there and dreamed, but the others became restless, and he descended the hill and joined the little boys, who were recovering fast, so that some were even ready to venture down into the caves again.

Then some hunters came back to report a deep well or pit, full of bones . . . yes, they had thought of the bones that filled The Cleft. It took them some time to admit they had flung stones down into the pit, and there had been an explosion: the stones had disturbed some pocket or store of bad air that had been waiting to explode. They were a little shame-faced, but not much, though Horsa was angry, and said there must not be more provocations of this kind. The noise of the explosion must have disturbed animals and birds. He was always telling them they were noisy and disruptive of the forest's ways.

Sometimes the hunters would be gone more than a day before finding game. And that was part of another difficulty. They all of them depended on the hunters for their food, to bring in animals to cook over the fires. But the young men did not hunt enough: they preferred the exploration of the caves and hills where they always found new systems of caves. The girls fetched fruit from the forest, a task which the boys found too tame, so there was always fruit. But there were not enough girls to feed them all, even though none was pregnant now and there were no babes to hinder them.

Horsa ordered a big hunt and again the carcasses dripped their fat into the fires and the flames licked up into the branches and in the morning the leaves hung brittle and pale.

The chroniclers did remark that if the women ever wanted to catch up with the men, they could easily follow them by the ashes of the fires, the bones, and the trees whose branches hung down marked by the flames.

They were talking about soon reaching the women's

shore, but this was because they were all hoping it would be soon. Hungers, not merely for sex but for the women themselves, were making them restless, impatient, and full of optimism. Did they miss the scoldings, the nagging? 'Maronna would say this, would say that,' Horsa might remark. She certainly would not have approved of their setting off the explosion in the pit which was like the real Cleft.

They decided to split again into two parties, one travelling through the forest, one in the caves beneath, if there were caves. And so they set off, Horsa again in command, though he was slow and awkward on his stick.

This part of their great journey is poorly recorded. One day must have been much like another. The initial confidence that set them off from the beach, where Horsa's tempting land could be seen, left them. And Horsa seemed to feel that every day on this last leg of their journey took him away from the pearly gleam of the horizon he longed for. He did not find a hill again from whence he could see the place, though he did see from an eminence a glitter and shine from a waterfall, so that he wondered if the flashes he had seen, that might have been lightning, had been in fact sun dazzling off water.

And meanwhile, what of the female shore, the women, of whom the men thought and spoke more and more? The women waited . . . and waited. For the return of . . . well, for one thing it was their children they wanted. Every one of the absent males was, after all, brother or son . . . but I don't dare use the word lover. We have to assume that the words 'I love you' were not likely to have been spoken, or heard – yet. 'I like you better than the others' – yes, permissible, I think. As we may hear one of our children, far from their men's or women's shape, say shyly to another, perhaps with a childish and even clumsy kiss on the cheek. I am not saying these so far-away and long-ago people were childish. I simply cannot 'hear', as I delve back into the past, 'I love you.'

'I miss you' . . . 'We miss them' . . . yes, I can hear that, easily.

Since Maronna had left Horsa at the start of his escapade . . . yes, I may hear *that* word easily enough – do I 'hear' 'Men are just grown-up children', which I am sure every male reader of this work has had thrown at him at moments of dissension with his wife – or lover? How easily I can write 'lover' here, of us . . . Since Maronna had seen Horsa last, apart from the occasional girls returning home because they found the men's ways too rough, not a word had been heard from the travellers. They might have walked off the edge of the world . . . but wait, there was no edge or limit to their world and it is so hard for us to imagine that, for us, who are so used to thinking of the boundaries of our great empire, which we know covers most of the world. Not a word. Surely the expedition could have spared someone to venture back and reassure the women? None of the women knew how far the men had gone, and had had no idea of how they had lingered on that distant beach where Horsa had dreamed of his pearly golden shore – and had become a cripple. The messenger would have to report Horsa's broken leg, and some casualties of boys lost to swamps and rivers; and, later, said that quite a few little boys were lost. Better, perhaps, that the women did not know.

Meanwhile the little boys, rejected for the adventure because they were too small, were growing up, and if far from their grown-up shapes, they were not really little children now. They were strong, taught by the waves, their playground. They complained a great deal, deprived of their playground in their forest and their right to run away from the women and find the men in the trees and grow up with them. They knew they could not do this: knew 'their place' was not theirs, and could not be until the men returned and fought the great dangerous pigs and cats and reclaimed their rightful home, the men's place. Without the hunters, the big boys, nothing could happen, and so the little boys, who were no longer so little, waited for the men, just as the women did, for their lives to become whole.

It was uncomfortable on the women's shores,

which had been tolerable when the boys took themselves off to the men in the trees. There were far too many in that space, and had been for a long time. One thing was slowly driving them all rather mad – there were no babies, and no prospect of any, for there were no pregnant women. The youngest infant was already walking. No crying babies, though little boys made enough noise. People were remembering old myths: surely things had been better when males had not been needed to make children? The moon, or the ocean, or even great fish had impregnated females, or even the spirit of The Cleft itself. Now women over-ready for mating sat around uselessly on the rocks and talked about the men. They waited, that was all.

When they talked of the men, and the missing boys, there was foreboding. They knew what a careless lot the men were. 'If they had to carry the babes swelling in their wombs, and then give birth in pain they wouldn't be so careless, risking life . . .' *'Don't you care about us, Horsa, don't you care?'*

They talked sometimes of specific boys, vulnerable in different ways. One was subject to bad coughs, another was not as strong as others, yet another slept badly and had nightmares. In the minds of these females were images or mental maps of these boys, their boys, and ghostly maternal hands slid over ghostly limbs, testing, measuring; though the bodies in question had grown beyond permitting others to handle already fiercely touch-me-not limbs – grown beyond their mothers, and far beyond babyhood. Perhaps some were dead? Premonitions darkened the thoughts of the women, who would weep for no reason, or wake suddenly from bad dreams. Of Brian, Big Bear, Runner, White Crow.

The littlest boys, who were no longer so little, bored and rebellious, took to swimming too dangerously, and to climbing the cliffs, so as to test themselves, and then some sneaked off in the old way to find adventure in the trees. Lookouts had to be set, half-grown girls who could run as fast as any boy, and could keep up with the boys. They had to intercept, catch the boys, and this became a game in its own right. This was to everybody's relief, for it used up a lot of energy, which otherwise would be put into dangerous games. Then these young girls, often perched in high places, able to see everything, not merely some venturesome little boys trying to dash past her, reported strange events. A mountain, not so far away, seemed to explode, in a way that left its summit jagged. One girl said she had actually seen, though from a distance that made it hard to be accurate, shapes in the trees not animal, and probably one of the men.

This set up a ferment and an impatience.

Impatience was becoming bad temper. A girl accused

another of sneaking off by herself to an assignment with one of the hunters, and then accusations became general. Yet no one had been sure of seeing one of the males. The shapes seen in the trees could have been bears, or cats, or any one of the big animals who went up trees. Maronna, usually at a distance from the women's arguments, now took a stand. What was going on was simply ridiculous. So she said. It was dangerous too. Quarrelling, and to the point of blows, surely this kind of thing was done by men, who enjoyed arguments and even fighting. Why, they even set up fights among themselves for the fun of it. Surely, she insisted – but her own voice was too high, was querulous – they knew that what was making them all so edgy and so ready to take offence was simply that their wombs had not been filled.

She stood on a rock that gave her height over the women and the boys and said, 'Look at us. There is not a filled womb among the lot of us. Look at our flat stomachs and our empty breasts. Surely we understand what is really speaking when we raise our voices and accuse others? This has never happened before: or there is no record of it. We need our men to return and fill our wombs. That is all. Surely we can wait patiently without behaving like little children . . .' And she wept. Of course, the boys did not understand this. Women had stomachs which grew in size, and then there was a crying baby and a flat stomach . . . they had known all this, had taken it for granted, but never thought about it.

'The girls can't have babies without us,' they concluded, and then were observed inspecting that part of their anatomy which had once, so very long ago now, made them Monsters.

Maronna, as bad-tempered and empty of purpose as any of them, swam far into the waves and thought that once long ago a wave could deposit a babe into a womb – or, at least, so the old tales said; and she swam around and among the rocks and thought: perhaps it could happen again.

And they all – the females – sat around under a full moon and told each other the ancient stories of how babes had once come into being because of strong moonlight. And perhaps, if they sat there long enough and stared long enough at the moon, then perhaps . . .

To put an end to the accusations of secret assignations with the men, Maronna told them that it was extremely unlikely the shapes they had seen were their men. If they were really so close, then they would have come running to them. Of course the men would be missing them as much as they longed for the men. The women knew that hunger for them ruled the men's lives, even if when they had achieved a mating they forget the women – until next time. There were many jokes made. Surely these were the earliest jokes on this subject ever made? I believe that we, living so long after, may safely transpose our jokes back to that past. After all, then as now, a male cannot hide it when a certain part of his anatomy hungers. Our togas and our robes are a great help, but those people could not conceal much under their skins and fish skins, their feathers and leafy aprons. Our bawdy plays in every bar or tavern rely a great deal on that part of our male anatomy. How could things have been different then? I believe the source of that laughter ringing down so many ages is simply this: the women nag and chide and criticise but they have to rely on a certain restlessness of what, long before then, made males be called Monsters. But . . . I digress. It is simply that I cannot believe that a certain type of joke, men's and women's, never existed, or could ever die out.

The boys, waiting for the men, having learned of their importance, examined themselves, drew conclusions, and began boasting – and joking – which added to the women's irritability.

Not far away, in fact so near the distance between Maronna and Horsa could have been covered in half a day's walking, the young men were going off in groups in all directions, returning at intervals only because Horsa insisted. Some hunters recognised a certain configuration of the trees and ran off to investigate. They might not have recognised The Cleft, which was close, or the shore, which continued from the women's shore and was like it, but as soon as they stood together in the glade which they all remembered, there was nothing hazardous in their planning. They had remembered the dangerous beasts, and had their weapons to hand. They stood silent under the trees which had looked over their childhood and there was nothing to spoil their memories but the three women they had brought with them, and who had protested at the men's insistence that they must come. The men wanted sex, and while it was time, so their natures told them, to mate, the women were reluctant and, to use our terms (and probably our ideas), coquettish. After all, none knew the end of their expedition would be so soon; they probably believed this journeying would go on and on, as it had done until now. Which meant that babies would be born as they travelled, and might die. Did they think like this? All the chronicles say is that the women 'denied the men their ease'.

In all the records we have there is never a complaint about the sexual demands of the boys, not even when there were many more males than females, even when occurred what we would call gang rape. We may interpret this as we like, and it seemed they may have made the attempt. The explanations all reflect bias. For instance, some of our stricter matrons think to refuse sex while pregnant is only right and proper. Some religious sects have fanciful reasons we need not go into here.

The hunters that day in the forest were regretting having dragged the girls along with them, who were noisily complaining that this was a dangerous place, and as usual the boys were not taking enough care. The boys were in fact looking out for, in particular, the pigs. The sheds and shelters that had been here were now wrecks; a platform built in a tree by presumably one of the children had collapsed under the weight of presumably, a great cat. Where a sow had wallowed, the water was running clear again but there was an underlay of churned mud, with a blurring of muddy water over it, and then clear water. It was not from the sow's wallow that a recent tenancy could have been deduced, but droppings, which were fresh enough to have the girls looking uneasily into the undergrowth.

'Why aren't they here?' the boys were muttering, looking about them and holding their weapons ready. The girls scorned: 'Oh, you are so stupid. They were here before because we were here, and now they will come again as soon as they know we have come back.'

The boys muttered that at the beginning of the occupation of the glade there were no animals, or not many, and the girls said, 'Of course they didn't come at once. They had never seen anything like us. They didn't know at the start that we are good to eat. And anyway we don't want to be here when they come.' And they began to cry.

'Why don't you run back to Horsa,' said the boys. 'You always spoil everything.'

'Why don't you just take us back to our place on the shore?'

This had not occurred to the boys. They could not remember now how easy it had been, moving back and forth from here to the shore. Their beautiful times here now seemed to them a long time ago, and their running back and forth was hazy in their minds. But they weren't going to admit this to the girls. 'Why should we? You know the way – then just run back yourselves.'

'But we are afraid, by ourselves. What about the animals?'

The boys were reluctant to show the girls they hardly knew where they were in relation to the women's place. Yet the girls had guessed this. How did they do this? It was uncanny, the ways the females seemed to read your mind.

 And that capacity certainly hasn't been lost! says your present historian.

'What is the matter with you?' the girls wanted to know. 'Why is it you never seem to know where you are?'

They were remembering how a group of the boys, including two of the present group, had gone round and round in a certain loop of the tunnel, not recognising the landmarks until a girl had said, 'Can't you see? We've been through this bit of tunnel more than once?'

And now the boys really did not seem to know where they were.

'Can't you see The Cleft?' a girl pointed out. And indeed, the great cliff of The Cleft stood up above the trees, not so far off.

The men stared. Yes, it is The Cleft. That meant . . . had Horsa seen it?

The males said they were hungry, and would hunt.

'I suppose you are going to make a fire,' said the girls. 'What a clever idea, it will bring all the animals here to us at once.'

This was what the boys wanted, and what the girls very much did not want. Meanwhile, the girls found some fruit near the clearing, and they all ate enough of it to keep hunger away. It got dark and the girls put themselves up a tree, while the boys squatted under the trunk, their weapons ready.

One girl said they must keep an eye on the boys, because they would probably sneak off without them, if they could. And when the first light came the boys were gone.

'Don't they care about us?' said the girls, wistfully

enough. And then they went on with a favourite topic, that the boys were so clumsy in relationships, so awkward much of the time, seemed to lack a sense, or senses.

The girls then made their way to their shore, very frightened, since they had no weapons. The paths and tracks were overgrown, and trees had fallen here and there. It was not a pleasant journey.

They reported to Maronna that the men, still led by Horsa, were not too far away, but the girls mustn't get their hopes up, because the men didn't seem to know how near home they were.

Meanwhile the three hunters made their way to Horsa, taking their time to stop for a likely cave mouth, or to climb a difficult tree, or to chase after a dangerous-looking boar.

From his anxious questioning, his reproaches, they did understand they had been away too long. Horsa had sent other youths after them, into the tunnels: wasn't that where they had said they were going? Yes, they had said that, but when they had seen those trees again, *their* trees, they had not been able to resist.

'And the girls are angry with us too,' they said, sulky, sounding like children. Well, they are not much more. How old? Fifteen? Sixteen? Less? They were at the age when we believe it is time for our young men to think about joining the army or finding a patron.

Horsa was a good bit older than the others, but probably still in his early twenties.

'The girls are so angry with us, they are so moody,' they grumbled.

Horsa said, grinning, that it was long past the time they should have visited the women.

'They'll only crab and complain.'

'And who was saying if he didn't have a girl soon he'd go mad?'

Grins all around. These bashful grins are the earliest we have records for. How much earlier than that did they appear? we have to wonder. The basis of all comedy, they are; we know, for instance, what the Greeks found funny. But so long ago, so very long?

'I don't want you to go off again,' said Horsa. 'You'll go off, and then the others will come back and go off. I want us all to be together and go together to the girls. If you've seen our old place in the forest, then the women are not far away.'

'Yes, and there is The Cleft.'

Horsa found it hard to recognise this old so well-known landmark from this angle. At last he saw it, and there was a moment of doubt.

Horsa did not look forward to telling Maronna about the lost boys. And the others had had a recent tongue-lashing from the girls and were reminded how very difficult girls could be.

'Is it all right if we go and hunt?' the boys demanded,

and promised they would come back by nightfall.

I would like to imagine a solicitousness in those young voices. After all, they had left Horsa alone for some days, when they had promised not to. Had he been lonely? – perhaps they wondered.

'Yes, go, but come back when the light goes.'

Was he lonely, left so often alone and part disabled, because of his crippled leg? May we use that word, and other words from our lexicons of feeling? We assume that because these people had shapes like ours, were so much like us, that they felt the same. Perhaps no one had taught them loneliness? Is that such a ridiculous question? Or sorrow? There is not much in the records, for instance, of love, the way we use the word, or jealousy – nothing about jealousy, yet it is so common an emotion that we may watch birds quarrelling over a mate. The whole region of specu-lation is difficult for me. It teases, challenges, and leaves me wondering. We know how our exemplars, the Greeks, *felt* – their plays tell us.

If those old long-ago people had written plays we would know how they felt. There is no record of them so much as making marks on bark or on stone. They told their histories into the ears of the Memories and perhaps never thought that when they said, for instance, 'Horsa longed for his "other" land,' that people coming so many ages later would not know what they meant by 'longing', 'wanting', 'dreaming'.

'Were you sad, Horsa?'

'Sad?'

'Well, let's try this. When you think about that magic shore of yours, what is it you feel about it? Do you think, "There will be my kind of people at last, and they will say, 'Horsa, there you are, why have you taken so long? We were waiting for you.'?" Is it that you feel you are excluded from some general happiness?'

'Happiness?'

When we send these shouts into the past, they have to be questions. But there need not be answers.

If I am sitting next to a person of my own generation, and I say, 'Do you remember?' – the words I use mesh with events in this person's memory, and the air between us is, as it were, alive and listening. Say the same words to someone of a younger generation and it is like throwing stones into the sea.

Questioning Horsa, nothing comes back.

Perhaps, if he could hear me, he might say, 'No, you don't understand. You see, I know everything there is to know about our land, every tree, plant, bird, animal. But that other shore I saw there, gleaming like a dawn. I know nothing about that place. *I have to know* – don't you understand that?'

Perhaps that is what he would say, and yes I do understand that, and a lot more about him he would not understand. But my questions are from an old

Roman reaching the end of his life – and we have no idea, none, about what they thought, or felt.

Names can help. We know that Maire and Astre – who were as remote to Horsa as he and his kind are to us – brought the heavens into their lives by using the names of stars. Horsa was the name of a star before it acquired Egyptian names, Greek names, our Roman names.

If we knew what that star meant then, perhaps we might hear Horsa speaking at last. Or imagine we did.

Horsa waited for his young men to return, and his thoughts were heavy and hard to bear. It says so in the stories. It was because of what he would have to tell Maronna. This was one occasion when he could not run off, find another valley, a new glade in the forest. It was not that he did not regret the little boys who had vanished into the caves. But he could not help thinking that wombs were quickly filled and then babies were born and – look, a new crop of babes. And so the sooner the men got to the women, the better.

Meanwhile he looked out over the top of the trees – he was on a little hill – and he gazed at The Cleft, which looked so different from this angle, and he saw white clouds coming out of The Cleft, and heard the thud-thudding of several explosions. He knew at once what had happened. Those mad men, his brave

young men, had been unable to resist throwing a
boulder or two down into the pit.

And now groups of the hunters, of those who could
not keep out of the caves, came running to Horsa,
and, too, the boys who had been rescued from the
well in the cave. They stood around Horsa, looking
at him, waiting for his anger, his recriminations, but
all he said was, 'And now it is time we went to the
women.'

Slowly, at first, they all set off, but Horsa could
not keep up and soon he was far behind, with the
rescued boys.

'Will Maronna be angry with us?' they asked, and
he said, 'Well, what do you think?'

The further they went, the more they could see the
damage that was done by the explosions. White lay
ever more thickly over the trees and then, when they
reached it, the rocky shore where the women would
be waiting for them. The powdered bones of so many
generations were making a thick layer from where
drifts of white went off into the air as the breezes
blew. And then there were the women, in the distance,
and the boys set up a howl, because they feared those
white ghosts who were wailing and crying.

In front of Horsa had pressed the young males,
but they were hanging back now, afraid of the
women. They were close together, for protection.
The sea breezes lifting the white powder from the

women made them look as if they were smoking. The Cleft that had dominated all that landscape was half its size, and it shed little avalanches of yet more white dust. The sea had a white crust and the waves lifted it, crinkling against the beach. The white looked solid enough to walk on. Some women trying to rid themselves of the white powder at the edge of the sea found themselves even more crusted thick and they were trying to rub the stuff off them, crying out in horror and rage. Yet a little further the sea was clear.

When Maronna saw Horsa, at first she did not recognise this limping man, and then she went for him, screaming, 'Why did you do it? The Cleft! You've killed The Cleft. Why?' She knew the men were responsible, and that meant Horsa was responsible. Her accusations were hysterical, her ugly screams distorted her white-streaked face.

'It's our place, you've destroyed our place.'

'But Maronna, there are better places. I keep telling you. There is a much better place a little further along. We've just passed it.'

'We've been here always, always. We are born here. You were born here. You were born in that cave up there.' And now she began to sob pitifully, her rage abating, and he loosely held her, and thought that he would never understand females. Why had Maronna, or some previous Maronna, not moved long ago?

This shore had always been cramped and crowded. And if they moved just a little way . . . it was a good thing The Cleft had been blown up if that meant the women would at last have a decent beach.

'Come on, Maronna, you can't stay here,' and he summoned his young men by pointing along the shore behind him. They understood him, because they had all many times discussed how foolish the women were not to move to a more spacious shore.

With his arm round Maronna, Horsa led the company, quite a large one we have to deduce, of the mateable women, who would soon be mothers again, and just behind them were the little boys rescued from the cave, as close to Maronna as they could get: they had forgotten, in all those months of being so much with men, that women did mean comfort, warmth, kindness. Behind them came the three girls who had run here from the forest: they had not told Maronna about the bad things on the trip. All the women wept and looked back at their desecrated shore. Then they were not looking back: the sea was no longer white, but blue with a white film, and then it was itself, its own colour. They had left the world of powdered bone behind. At once all the women plunged into the sea, their element, their mother – at least so some of them believed – and they emerged glistening like healthy seals. And here we have another little clue as to how they looked. 'They stood wringing out their long hair.' The males stood watching, and then at once began the long-awaited mating. Maronna and Horsa went ahead down the beach. For how long? For how far? 'It was quite a distance' is what we have. And, 'A comfortable walk for healthy women.'

Horsa pulled Maronna to stand with him on rocks so similar to the ones they had left behind – for ever. Rocks, and rock pools and lively splashing waves and beyond them a long shining beach of clean white sand: there was no beach at the women's old shore.

'And look,' said Horsa, pointing up at the cliffs that overshadowed this beach. 'Caves. Just as good as the ones you used.'

Maronna, who after all had all the qualities that enabled her to rule the women, stood silent, looking at the beach: she understood very well what advantages were there.

The rescued little boys, having washed themselves, came running up to Maronna and Horsa.

But, as we know, there were few of them.

Maronna stepped back from the shelter of his arms and said, 'Where are the other boys? When are they coming?'

And here it was, the dreaded moment. Horsa stood in front of his accuser, head bowed, his arms loose at his sides, palms towards her – and this posture told her what she would hear. Horsa trembled as he stood, and his crutch, the stick, shook too.

Maronna was already tearing her wet hair with both hands. Remember, she usually had hair 'piled on top of her head'. Now it flowed down, excepting for where the white powder clogged it. She tugged and tore at it, trying to make this pain bad enough to still the anguish she felt.

'Where are they, Horsa, where?'

He shook his head and she screamed, 'They are dead, then? You have killed our little boys. Oh, I might have known. What did I expect, really? You are so careless, you don't care . . .' And so they stood, facing each other, on the edge of the splendid beach which would soon house all the women and the children and the visiting men too. She was so full of anger, while he stood there, limp, guilty, in the wrong. Maronna screamed and went on screaming, and at last her voice went hoarse, and she stood silent, looking, but really looking at him. He was trembling, he was limp with the grief he now genuinely did feel, because her agony of grief was telling him what an enormity he had committed. And she saw this, understood it. She saw, and really took in that pitiful leg, the shrivelled, twisted leg.

Tenderness is not a quality we associate easily with young men. Life has to beat it into us, beat us softer and more malleable than our early pride allows. Horsa saw Maronna, as he had not before. Perhaps he had felt her more than seen her, as an always accusing

257

critical presence. He saw this trembling girl, still streaked with the white powder, though her face was washed with tears. She was in such distress, so help- less: he grew up in that moment, and stood forward to take her in his arms as she opened her arms to him. 'Poor child,' she was whispering. 'Poor boy,' she crooned, and now he broke down and wept and the great Horsa was a little boy again. It was sweet, yes, I am sure I may safely say that. To become a little child in your mother's arms, petted and forgiven . . . and for all we know, or they knew, Maronna was Horsa's mother.

The greater the capitulation to the female, the greater there will be the recoil: and I have to write this, too. Who has not seen it, known it, understood?

There, in Maronna's arms, loved and forgiven, somewhere in Horsa's restless mind had started the thought: Tell her about the wonderful place I found, yes I will. She'll want to see it too, I am sure of it. She will understand, yes, she'll come with me, we'll go together, I'll make a ship better than any we've made, and we'll land together on that shore and . . .

I had not expected to say any more on this subject, for one thing I am old now, and the scholarly life is not easy for me. But the eruption of Vesuvius has made me think again about The Cleft, and its comparatively modest explosion. Vesuvius killed people at a great distance from it, as far away as Pompeii, and it seems a noxious powder was the cause. Nothing survives its touch. But The Cleft too had poisonous fumes, and its outburst of whitish powder killed no one. Yet The Cleft was quite close to the shore where the women and children were. This in itself must surely provoke questions? There is a great deal it seems we do not know, though we Romans like to behave as if we know everything. Pliny, my old friend, was in pursuit of knowledge – and died for his efforts. For some days the sea near the women's shore washed in waves crusted with bone dust, on rocks that acquired a hard patina which did not disappear, so the records say. And a little further down the coast the sea ran in blue and clean. A pretty minor affair, the destruction of The Cleft – and yet it leaves questions that in their own way are as difficult as the ones we ask over the great volcano, which we must assume will one day blow again.

The white rocks near The Cleft looked as if they had been covered with guano, and it occurs to me now to wonder if a careful search around all the coasts of the islands of our sea might reveal once whitened rocks that we would agree were the site of that old story, Clefts and Monsters. But the outburst of Vesuvius tells us we may not assume permanence for the coastlines of islands or even the islands themselves. And suppose we did decide that this set of bleached rocks was what we were after – this would be of only a sentimental interest. Those historians – and they called themselves so, seeing themselves as the recorders of the very long ago – wrote from their villages in the forests as of chronicles of events that had their end when The Cleft exploded. (Villages – how many? Where? Of how many people?) The village historians wrote with charcoal sticks on the inside of bark. They no longer spoke their stories into receiving ears. None of these old bark records remain, but what followed them, marks on reed scrolls, still remain – a few. The explosion of The Cleft is both the end of a tale and the beginning of the next. Historians who wrote long ages before me agreed on that – and so let it be.